Mills & Boon

BEST SELLER ROMANCE

A chance to read and collect some of the best-loved novels from Mills & Boon—the world's largest publisher of romantic fiction.

Every month, three titles by favourite Mills & Boon authors will be re-published in the *Best Seller Romance* series.

A list of other titles in the *Best Seller Romance* series can be found at the end of this book.

Roberta Leigh

FACTS OF LOVE

MILLS & BOON LIMITED
15–16 BROOK'S MEWS
LONDON W1A 1DR

First published in Great Britain 1978 by Mills & Boon Limited

© Roberta Leigh 1978

Australian copyright 1978
Philippine copyright 1979
Reprinted 1979
This edition 1985

ISBN 0 263 75191 0

Set in Linotype Plantin 10 on 11 pt.
02–0785

Made and printed in Great Britain by Richard Clay (The Chaucer Press) Ltd, Bungay, Suffolk

CHAPTER ONE

THERE was a knock at the door and Paula Grayson looked up from some documents as Mrs Maxwell, a quiet, efficient woman who had been her father's secretary until his death three years ago, and was now her own, came in.

'Yes?' Paula queried.

'I just wanted to remind you that you have an editorial meeting in ten minutes. I'm not sure if you're going to the Board room for it or having it here.'

'Here.' Paula swivelled round in her chair. 'It isn't a full meeting; I'm only seeing Ron Smith. Which reminds me, how's the whisky supply?'

'I'm sure Mr Smith would appreciate the association!' Mrs Maxwell crossed to the rosewood cupboards that lined the far wall and opened one of them. A lavish array of bottles met her eye. 'Enough to launch a ship,' she stated.

'As long as there's enough to launch Ron Smith,' Paula smiled.

Mrs Maxwell smiled back, thinking how different her employer looked when she relaxed. If only she could be encouraged to relax more. If she did, she would have no difficulty in finding the right man to love her. Not that there was a shortage of men in Paula Grayson's life; on the contrary. But they all had their eye on the main chance: in love with all she could offer them materially and uncaring of all she had to offer emotionally; so eager to share her power—possibly even to usurp it—that they did not see her as a woman.

And what a woman she was! Schooled by a Titan of a father, she had now become a Titan in her own right. A newspaper tycoon who had inherited a country and turned

it into an empire. It was unfortunate that in the process
of doing this, her agressive instincts had been sharpened to
the detriment of her feminine ones. But femininity had not
been an asset which Samuel Grayson had cherished, and he
had modelled his daughter in his own image instead of
allowing her to develop in her own. Mrs Maxwell sighed
as she remembered the bright-eyed child he had first
brought to the office. How quickly she had given way to
the determined schoolgirl and even more determined teenager. But determined only in one thing: to show her father
she was as capable and intelligent as the son he had longed
for and never had.

'What's wrong with you?' Paula asked. 'You look as if
you've lost a pound and found a penny.'

It aptly described the way Mrs Maxwell felt about her
employer, but she knew that to say such a thing would not
be favourably received. Paula Grayson looked and acted as
if she were well content with her life, and it did not behove
an employee to suggest otherwise. Yet she had to say something of what she felt; not to have done would have been
dishonourable to herself.

'I was just wishing you would take things more easily,'
she hedged.

'I'd die of boredom.'

'Not if you had a husband and children.'

'I knew you'd get on to that subject,' Paula said with
mock severity, and went into the small but beautifully
appointed bathroom that lay off her office. She glanced at
herself in the mirror, patted her hair into place and dabbed
some powder on her nose before returning to her desk.

She was a tall girl, well-developed and beautifully pro-
portioned, and moved with the unconscious grace of a
tigress. Her colouring was tigerish too: lightly tanned skin,
oval-shaped brown eyes with flecks of gold to make them
look lighter, and thick, tawny brown hair, worn long and
casual.

As usual, she wore a simple shirt dress, tightly belted at the waist and with the sleeves pushed up carelessly. A heavy gold bracelet encircled one wrist and a thick gold necklace lay upon her throat. It was the last gift she had received from her father and a day rarely passed when she did not wear it. The heavy gold suited her personality, its barbaric design giving a hint of that part of her character which she was always careful to keep in check. It had been given to few men to see her with her defences down and of those, only two were now alive: her lawyer, who had been the family one for as long as she could remember, and Guy Ardrey, legal adviser to the company, who still hoped to persuade her to marry him.

She swivelled round in her chair and stared out of the window at the roof tops several stories below her eye level. The offices of Grayson Publications towered above its neighbours in the same way that its newspapers towered above its rivals. The knowledge made her proud yet afraid. It was awesome to know she was solely in command. If only she had been the son her father had so desperately wanted! Heaven knows she had tried hard enough.

She swivelled back to face the room, though she did not see it, her thoughts still preoccupied with the past and that morning, a year before his death, when her father had suddenly tweaked off the velvet band she had worn to keep her hair away from her face and, watching it fall in an amber cloud to her shoulders, had abruptly said he wanted her to look more feminine.

'You're a beautiful girl and it's time you acted like one,' he had added, and had followed this statement by taking her to Paris and buying her a wardrobe fit for a queen.

But the new mantle which he dropped upon her shoulders had not fitted Paula easily. She had spent too many years as heir to the Grayson throne for her now to become its heiress. Besides, her father still wanted her to be forceful and driving, and she had found it impossible to play two parts. Because of that, she had quickly reverted to the part she had played since childhood. The pretty clothes were pushed to the back of her wardrobe and were replaced by her usual tailored ones; the bottles of make-up lay untouched in her bathroom and the flagons of scent were used with such restraint that their effect was minimal. Only her new hairstyle had remained: a reminder of the girl she might have been, had she had a brother whose role she had not been expected to assume.

Occasionally her father commented on her reluctance to change her appearance, saying how much he enjoyed seeing her look pretty, and pleading with her not to totally discard her new image.

'I'm too old for images,' she had said, almost angrily, when he had broached the subject for the third time in as many weeks. 'What's bred in the mind comes out in the matter!'

'Are you saying I've indoctrinated you?'

'I'm saying that you moulded me into thinking and acting like a man, and that you can't expect me to change into a frilly little girl just because it now suits you.'

'You could never be a frilly little girl,' he had snorted. 'Though I admit I want to see you acting like a woman. It's time you began thinking of marriage, Paula. I'm not getting any younger and I'd like to——'

'See a grandson, since you only had a daughter,' she had cut in.

'Don't use the word only,' he had said quickly.

She had not answered him, suddenly seeing the reason for the trip to Paris, the desire to re-fashion her. In the same way that her father had moulded her into his aggressive right arm, he was now trying to remould her into someone who would present him with the male heir that her own birth—and mother's death—had prevented him from having.

'It won't work, Father. You can't change me at this

stage of my life. I've learned to use my brain to get what I want, and I've no intention of discarding it or hiding it.'

'What's one thing got to do with the other?'

'Everything. Men don't like women in control. You know that. And they certainly don't love them! That's why you took me to Paris, wasn't it? You were hoping that a feathered hat could make me look like a feather-brain! Well, it won't. I'm what you made me, and you're stuck with it.'

'Does that mean you don't want to get married?'

'Of course it doesn't. As you've just said, what's one thing got to do with the other? But it will have to be to a man who sees me as I am, not as someone I would like to be.'

Within a week of this conversation her father was dead; victim of a coronary that struck without warning. Paula no longer had time to worry about her femininity or the plans her father had had for her. She was too busy fighting to retain control of her empire and to ward off the take-over bidders—all masculine—who assumed that without a man at the helm, the carefully groomed heir would collapse into an heiress ready to sell out.

Never, she had vowed to herself. It's time Fleet Street had a woman in the chain of command. If Paris and Washington can, then so can London. And London is going to start with *me*.

The start had not been difficult—momentum carrying on the company for several months—but then cracks and crevasses began to appear, and all Paula's acumen was called into play. Each move she made could have been a disaster, but was the exact opposite. Using flair and intuition—something she could never have done in her father's lifetime —she chose her own team and built them up to be the most powerful one in the industry. They had had their share of problems but far more than their share of successes, and though the bids to buy out Grayson Publications still came in with regularity, they came in with respect and envy, not as lifelines pushed out to a hapless female.

In less than two years the share value of the Group increased by twenty per cent. They launched a woman's magazine and a family one, and she pinched Ron Smith away from one of her rivals to become editor of their own revamped Sunday paper, a move that had met with the opposition of the entire Board, but which she had pushed through by dint of persuasion. The almost immediate upward swing in sales of the *Sunday Recorder* had been all the justification she had needed. From then on the Board did not argue with her when she wanted any changes made on the editorial side.

Another eighteen months passed. Their success now had the consolidation of time, and Paula's position was unassailable. Yet for some reason she could not define, she was dissatisfied with herself. The knowledge came upon her gradually, filtering through every aspect of her life until she could no longer ward it off. Intelligence warned her that it was age regretting lost youth, and though she knew she could never bring back those years, she could not prevent herself from wondering how best to use the ones that remained for her.

She ran her hands through her hair, momentarily disarraying the heavy strands. Was marriage the solution she was looking for? And if it was, how could she meet the right man? It was hard to believe that with more than a thousand employees at her command, she had never met anyone who had made her heart beat faster. Even on the rare occasions when she had felt a flutter, she had soon discovered that the man regarded her not as a woman he wanted to protect but as someone strong enough to protect *him*! She supposed that strong-minded men did exist, but was rapidly coming to the conclusion that even if she eventually met one, it would lead to more friction than harmony. After all, there could not be two bosses in a marriage, and to hope for a partner who could control as well as defer was looking for the impossible.

She was still engrossed in her thoughts when Ron Smith, the editor of the *Sunday Recorder*, came in. She motioned him to help himself to a drink and he did so and came to sit in front of her: a plump man, not yet thirty, with a mild manner that hid North Country aggressiveness.

'Our espionage series is still putting up our circulation,' she said. 'I've just had the figures sent to me and we're ten per cent better than last Sunday—and that was ten per cent higher than the week before.'

'I knew it would be a winner. And we aren't finished yet, either. We've just touched the tip of the iceberg.'

'That's what I wanted to talk to you about. If you're sure you can find more grist for the mill, then——'

'No doubt of it,' he interpolated. 'We've got enough material for another six weeks—and that's only the first layer. We could run the series for a year if we wished.'

Her eyebrows rose. 'I'm surprised you can dig up so much dirt on industrial espionage. I know it's there, but I hadn't realised its ramifications.'

'I don't see why. The bigger the business, the bigger the profit. And big profits encourage thievery. You insure your jewellery and paintings, don't you?'

'Yes, but——'

'And that's what public companies do—often with the same lack of success. Except that when *they* get ripped off, it can cost 'em millions. Years of research and millions of pounds can go into the discovery of a new process of manufacture, a new drug, a different product—and one worm in a barrel can make it all worthless.'

Paula said nothing, though she was amused by the way Ron Smith had jumped on to his soapbox and harangued her.

'With your permission,' he said, 'I'd like to start naming names.'

'You don't need my permission for that,' she replied. 'You need the lawyers'.'

'If they know you're behind me they'll be more venturesome.'

'I don't want a libel action,' she warned.

'There won't be any. I've checked and double-checked every name I intend to use. This Sunday I'm going for the detergents. Daybright & Sons got hold of a new formula belonging to Weaver Brothers and planned to launch it as their own.'

'Under what name?'

'They never gave it one. The product was killed before it came out. When Weavers discovered their formula had been pinched, they infiltrated someone into Daybright and——'

'Stole it back?'

'Better than that. They re-jigged some of the equations so that Daybright spent three months trying to discover why the wonderful bleach they'd pinched turned everything pink!'

Paula laughed. 'Did they manage it?'

'Eventually. But by then, Weavers had put the *bona fide* one on the market.'

'And who are the people you want to name?'

'The man who passed the information over from Weavers. A man called Rossiter. He's been with Weavers since he came down from Cambridge. He's next in line for the top job on their scientific side.'

'He won't get it if you name him.'

'That's why I'm asking for your permission. Rossiter's bound to have a go at us. I can soft-pedal on it if you like or I can go all out to get him.'

'If you're certain he's guilty and can prove it, then do as you wish—after you've cleared it with the lawyers.' Paula swung her chair from side to side, a habit of hers when she was excited or over-alert. 'I've told you before, Ron, when I put someone in charge, I expect them to take

charge. As long as you're clear with the legal department....'

'I am.' Ron Smith stood up. 'Thanks, Miss Grayson. I'll
go ahead.'

Alone again, Paula turned her attention back to the
documents on her desk and was still studying them when
Guy Ardrey telephoned. Apart from being lawyer to the
company, he was also her closest male friend. Her closest
friend period, she thought as she said hello to him, for
she had never had time to make friends among her own
sex. Neither time nor inclination; and inclination, she
decided, had been the guiding factor. In general she had
found women envious and suspicious of her, and though
she knew that one day she might regret the lack of a
womanly ear in which to confide, she had been too busy
to try to rectify it. Now of course she was too old to do so.
She pulled a face. This was the second time today that she
had thought of herself as too old to do something. Was
it because her birthday was looming on the horizon?
Twenty-eight—two years away from thirty. The thought
was frightening and she refused to think of it.

'Anything wrong, Guy?' she asked, her voice husky yet
lilting. 'One of the loveliest things about you is your
voice,' Guy had once said, and she still remembered the
compliment.

'I rang to remind you we're going to the opera tonight.
I'll collect you at seven.'

'Good.' She put down the receiver, never one to waste
words. Another unfeminine trait, she decided, and vowed
that next time she would chat to him for a little longer.

In order to remain her friend he had taken the rough
with the smooth. More rough than smooth lately, she admitted, for she was finding it increasingly difficult to maintain her interest in him. But he was no different from the
way he had always been: the difference lay within herself
and her state of restlessness.

Perhaps she needed a holiday. A month on a sun-drenched island with a blond Adonis might work wonders. It might also work havoc. She glanced round quickly, as if afraid someone might guess her thoughts. A new hat was a far safer proposition, though nowhere near as satisfying. She pondered on both ideas and then decided to take herself to the hairdressers instead.

It was the best solution.

CHAPTER TWO

SITTING in Christopher's Mayfair salon, Paula decided to be more venturesome.

'I feel I need a change of personality,' she announced, 'so you'd better cut my hair.'

'I love your personality, Miss Grayson,' the young man replied, 'and I've not intention of cutting your hair.' He grinned at her through the mirror: a perky Cockney whose magic scissors had made him the rage of London for the past four years.

'I don't believe it,' she stated. 'A hairdresser who doesn't have scissor-fingers? Miracles never cease!'

'It wouldn't suit you to look like a shorn lamb,' he explained. 'You're the wolfish type.'

Her laugh was warm and clear. 'A vixen, you mean?'

He laughed too, as he picked up a heavy tress. 'I'll keep it the same length but I'll re-shape it. I've been wanting to do so for the past year, but you wouldn't let me.'

'Everything comes to those who wait.'

'What's come to you, Miss Grayson?'

She was startled and looked into his eyes via the mirror. Old age, she nearly said in reply, until she realised how self-pitying it might sound.

'A sense of adventure,' she lied. 'I feel a new woman and I want to look like one.'

The first sight of herself, an hour later, was a disappointment. Her hair looked exactly the same as when she had come in: thick and long, it fell from a side parting only a little higher than she normally wore it. She turned to look for a hand mirror and only then appreciated the difference: where before her hair had hung heavily to her shoulders, it now swung and lifted with every movement she made, drawing the eye to its lustrous sheen and tawny colour.

'It's very sexy,' Christopher said.

'You think so?'

'I know so. And I'm a better judge of a sexy woman than you are. And you *are*,' he reiterated.

She lifted her eyebrows. 'The one thing I've never considered myself is sexy.'

'You should hear what the girls in the salon say about you. They call you the sleeping tigress.'

She was taken aback. 'I'm not sure if that's a compliment!'

'It's meant as one.' He walked with her to the exit and helped her off with her smock. Casually he eyed her dress. 'Why don't you go to Robina? Her clothes are fabulous.'

'I'm not the frilly type,' Paula said decisively.

'Robina doesn't go in for frills. You should give her a try. Her place is in Davis Mews. You can't miss it—it's the building painted pink.'

'I'll do my best to miss it,' Paula said, and heard Christopher laugh as she left the salon.

Walking to her car she was extremely conscious of her hair swaying with every step she took, but by the time she mounted the steps of her St John's Wood home, she had become used to it and decided she liked it.

She was waiting for Guy half an hour before he was due to arrive and tried to look forward to her evening with him. Instead she found herself thinking of Ron Smith and the present series they were running in the *Recorder*. The sales were excellent and the rest of the articles should increase them further. After that would come the problem of maintaining them.

Voices sounded in the hall and she looked around as Guy came in. As always he squeezed her hands gently and kissed her on the cheek.

'Dear Paula, you never keep me waiting.' This was his standard greeting too.

'I think we've time for a drink before we leave,' she said.

Taking it as an invitation, he went to the sideboard and poured a sherry for her and a gin and tonic for himself.

'You're looking unusually charming, Paula.'

He came back to the electric fire glowing in the grate. Central heating made it unnecessary but it gave the room a spurious air of being more lived in. If I stayed home more often, she thought, it wouldn't be spurious. I should do more entertaining here; use the library as an office instead of always rushing to Fleet Street; cultivate friends in other professions. I should also stop being so damned introspective, she warned herself. If I'm like this because I'm approaching twenty-eight, what am I going to be like when I'm approaching thirty?

'I like your dress,' Guy added. 'Is it new?'

'Good heavens, no. Just an old black one.'

'Only *you* would dare to describe a Valentine that way!'

She smiled and, watching him sip his drink, wondered why her heart refused to beat faster at the sight of him. Was it because she was too used to him—he had been her escort since she was in her teens—or because she saw him as a family friend rather than a future lover or husband? Not lover, she amended. Guy would never want that sort of relationship with her. He might have a girl-friend tucked away in Maida Vale or Chelsea—someone pretty and not too bright who would be delighted by his smooth charm—but when it came to herself, she was certain he saw her in terms of marriage; of the founding of a new dynasty to run the Grayson empire.

Abruptly she set down her glass and rose. 'Let's go, Guy. I hate rushing.'

He helped her on with her fur jacket and they went into the hall. At six foot three he topped her by almost a head, though she rarely noticed his height, for he was slimly built and did not exude any obvious masculinity. Guy took delight in understatement. Come to think of it, she had never heard him raise his voice beyond his normal, modulated tones. In the light of the wall brackets his pale skin had a warmer colour, though his eyes remained pale grey and his hair a lightish brown. It was the way he always wore it, and she knew an irrational desire to disarray the smooth strands. How surprised he would be if she did so! As he opened the front door he turned to her and noticed her smile.

'What's the joke, my dear?'

'I was thinking I've never seen you untidy,' she said candidly.

'I'm tidy by nature. From the moment I was born I was doomed to be Nanny's little pet and head boy of the school!'

She laughed, a warm sound that gave more indication of her true character than she realised. 'You're in a good humour tonight, Guy.'

'I thought I was always good-humoured?'

'Tonight you're even more so.'

'You're more so too. The trouble is I'm not sure what's caused the more so.' He opened the car door for her and watched as she climbed in. 'If it isn't a new dress, what is it?'

'A new hair-style.'

'Ah, I knew it was something.' He took the wheel and set the car in motion. 'It looks the same,' he said, glancing at her quickly, 'yet it isn't.'

'Do you like it?'

'Very much. But I liked it before, too.'

'I felt I needed a change.'

'We all need a change from time to time.' He negotiated his way through the traffic. 'I wish you'd give some more thought to us—our future together. I know I keep asking you the same question, but I still can't see why you won't get engaged to me.'

'Because I'm not in love with you. I'm fond of you, Guy, but that isn't enough for marriage.'

'You'd love me once I was your husband.'

'How can you be sure?'

'Because I know you. You've been independent for so long you're afraid to commit yourself to any one person.' He took his hand from the wheel and caught both of hers that were resting on her lap. 'You've also been alone too long. I should have insisted on marrying you soon after your father died.'

'You couldn't have insisted,' she said. 'I'm my own mistress.'

'And not likely to be mine.'

Surprised, she swivelled round on him. 'You've never asked me!'

'Because I want you as my wife and I'm prepared to wait. It's just that occasionally—like tonight when you look so lovely—I become impatient. Think about us, Paula. You aren't in love with anyone else and I know I'm the right man for you.'

'Don't rush me, Guy.'

'Hardly that,' he protested. 'We've known each other ten years.'

'Don't remind me! Do you know I'll be twenty-eight in a couple of weeks?'

'All the more reason to think of marriage.'

'I have been thinking about it,' she said, but forbore to add that it hadn't been to him.

They took their seats in the stalls a few moments before the curtain went up, and once it did, Paula forgot everything in the joy of listening to *Don Giovanni*. As the curtain came down for the first interval she wondered how she would react if a man like the Don came into her life and if she would ever, like poor Donna Anna, become so besotted over him that she would never see him for his true worthlessness.

'Care for a drink?' Guy asked and, at her nod, led her up the aisle towards the bar. It was extremely crowded and hot and he suggested they went upstairs. Here it was equally crowded, but they immediately saw a group of people they knew and Guy led her over to them, pleased when he saw they already had several bottles of champagne and glasses set out on the table in front of them. Paula was immediately given a drink and listened idly to the conversation, wishing Guy had not brought her over here, for the men were partners in a stockbroking firm and anxious to make a good impression on her, while their wives appeared typical of their background, being well dressed but vacuous.

What a critical bitch I am, she thought, and forced an attentive look to her face as she made a pretence of listening to what was being said. She heard the first bell ring and with a feeling of relief looked in Guy's direction. He was deep in conversation with one of the men and she knew he would remain talking until the final bell went. They would probably have to come up here during the second intermission too, she thought irritably, and decided she would spend it in her seat.

'I'll meet you downstairs, Guy,' she said, and with a nod, pushed her way towards the entrance.

A woman knocked against her and she was forced back. The heel of her shoe pressed down hard on someone's foot and she half turned to apologise. The owner of the foot grunted inaudibly and moved alongside her, though he seemed immersed in his own thoughts. They reached the head of the stairs simultaneously and were both reflected in the huge mirror that covered the wall ahead of them: a

sombrely dressed woman with shining, tawny hair and a
well built man, not much taller, in evening clothes and a
simple, unfrilled white shirt. He was so intent on reaching
the ground floor that he looked neither to right nor left as
he pushed his way forward. A group of people came up the
stairs, forcing him against the handrail. His shoulder, solid
as iron, knocked into Paula and almost sent her sprawling.

'Please,' she gasped. 'Do you think you could let me get
downstairs in one piece?'

Instantly he stopped in his tracks and steadied her. 'I'm
terribly sorry.' His voice was as incisive as his manner. 'But
I've only just remembered a call I promised to make before
leaving the office, and if I don't do it within the next five
minutes, it will be too late.'

'I should have guessed you weren't rushing to get back
to your seat in case you missed the next act!'

'That too,' he said.

'Then push on!'

He smiled and moved ahead and she followed more
slowly, watching him until he disappeared among the
crowd.

The second bell rang and she went into the auditorium,
reaching her seat at the same moment as a slightly breathless Guy joined her.

'I take it you won't want to spend the next interval with
Dick Benton?' he murmured.

'Was I as obvious as that?'

'You have a habit of not hiding your feelings.'

'You make me sound rude.'

'You don't mean to be. It's just your way.'

The remark, instead of mollifying her, disturbed her,
making her seem to be careless of other people's feelings,
which she wasn't. The trouble was she had never been able
to simulate. If she did not like someone, she could not
hide the fact. It had not mattered to her so far, though it
might have been a different story had she been obliged to

make her own way in life instead of having her path cleared for her by her father. What would I have achieved on my own? she wondered, but before she could find the answer, the music for the second act began.

During the next interval she and Guy remained downstairs standing by the outer doors to get some fresh air. She had her jacket around her shoulders and, after a moment, suggested they went and stood on the pavement. Other members of the audience were doing the same and she and Guy ambled down the road. It was an unusually mild night for February, with a light breeze almost reminiscent of spring.

It was only when they were retracing their steps that she saw the man she had bumped into earlier. He was standing by the brightly lit entrance with another couple, older than himself, and was deeply engrossed in conversation with them. Although only average in height, he had such an erect carriage and broad shoulders that he appeared to be taller. Indeed, had he not bumped into her earlier in the evening, she would have assumed him to be six foot, instead of several inches below it. He had a craggy but handsome face, with a firm nose and a thin-lipped mouth, wide and curving slightly as he spoke. Because his head was slightly bent she could not see his eyes, but he was gesticulating with his hands and she noticed they were large, with strong wrists on which she glimpsed a spattering of black hair. An extremely masculine man, she thought, and involuntarily glanced at Guy who, by contrast, appeared even sleeker than usual.

'Do you know that man?' he asked.

'No. What makes you ask?'

'The way you were looking at him.'

'I trod on his foot when I was leaving the crush bar.'

As if aware he was being watched, the man turned and glanced at her, though the movement could well have been caused by his companions' decision to move into the

theatre. Together they all went towards the main door and
once again Paula found the stranger beside her, though
this time he stepped aside to let her precede him.

'I won't step on your foot this time,' she said with a
slight smile.

'Good,' he replied crisply, and then turned immediately
to speak to his elderly companion in fluent German.

Paula coloured. She was not used to being so swiftly
ignored. Putting her hand on Guy's arm, she smiled up at
him without hearing what he said, and continued to smile
until they had taken their seats. What a fool she had been
to make that remark about treading on his foot! He had
probably seen it as a desire to speak to him again. Annoyance engulfed her and she made a conscious effort to stop
thinking about him. Perhaps he was a foreigner and afraid
of being thought familiar. His German was certainly fluent
enough to be his native tongue. That could also account for
his abrupt manner towards her. Germans were usually punc-
tilious over introductions and he would not expect a woman
he met at the opera to suddenly turn and speak to him.

All at once the incident became amusing. Had he really
thought she was trying to pick him up? He was the last
sort of man who would arouse that instinct in her. She
could as easily see herself flirting with a bulldog! The
allusion seemed apt, for he had the same pugnacious quality.
The curtains swung back and thankfully she put him from
her mind.

CHAPTER THREE

Of all the days in the week, Paula enjoyed Sunday the best. She breakfasted in bed and remained there while she read all the papers, her own and those of her English and foreign rivals. Invariably she jotted down notes which, the following day, would become memoranda sent to various of her editors. It was amazing how often one found bright ideas from glancing at other publications. The series on industrial espionage had come to her after looking at a particularly lurid story in a French tabloid.

She picked up the *Sunday Recorder* and settled to read it. Its news was factual with no political bias and its features bright and informative, written to appeal to the middle market. But its espionage series was written by Ron Smith himself and each article had been hard-hitting. Here was the stuff from which spy films and murder mysteries were made: real-life whodunits with stolen formulas taking the place of stolen government secrets and somebody else's detergent lying on the bathroom floor instead of a body. Ron had excelled himself in this week's episode and Jack Rossiter must be wishing himself a million miles away.

How had Ron managed to dig up so many facts? She had no doubt that each one was true, for he was too astute an editor to lie over salient points. She skimmed through the episode again. It was incredible that Rossiter had put his job at such risk. Hadn't he realised that if he were found out it would destroy his career? Still, when it came to making extra money—and large amounts at that—people became so greedy that they disregarded the risks. Unhappily he was being made to see them now, and after today would have a great deal to answer for.

The telephone rang and she picked it up, knowing that

only a handful of people had her private number. It was sure to be Guy, checking to confirm his lunch date with her and to ask if she had seen the *Recorder*. But in this she was wrong, for his first words were about the article she had just been reading.

'I've had Rossiter's lawyer on to me already,' he added. 'He's demanding that we take the *Recorder* off the news-stands immediately.'

'What a hope!'

'I told him it was out of the question,' he agreed.

'Particularly since two million have already been de-livered on to people's doorsteps,' she added. 'I suppose Rossiter's screaming libel?'

'That's putting it mildly. His lawyer's threatening to throw the book at us.'

'Ron Smith assured me every single word of it was true.'

'If he's lying it could cost us a packet.'

'Of course he isn't lying. He knows I'd crucify him if he were.' Paula glanced at the clock on her bedside table. 'I'll see you at noon, Guy.'

She had hung up before she remembered her vow not to end a conversation so abruptly. But it was too late to do anything about it now and she picked up the receiver again and dialled Ron Smith. He must have been expecting her call, for he lifted the telephone before it had given one ring.

'I take it you know about Rossiter's lawyer?' she said at once.

'No. But I can imagine.'

'You *did* check all your facts, didn't you?'

'Every word. I'm a professional editor, Miss Grayson, not a professional idiot. What are you going to do about the lawyer?'

'Nothing. If Rossiter threatens action we'll make it plain we can back everything we've said.'

With Ron Smith's assurance on this still ringing in her

ears, Paula lay in the bath and relaxed. She was not going to let Guy talk about the article when they met. She would set back lunch an hour and take him for a walk in the park. It was another unusually mild winter's day and she felt in need of exercise. Afterwards they would listen to music or watch television. Do anything, in fact, except discuss business.

The day passed in the way she had planned, and when she went to bed she felt considerably more unwound than for a long while. Only the question of whether she had a future with Guy still nagged at her, but it was one which she could not answer and she decided not to worry about it. One thing she must never do was to marry out of boredom or because she could not face a life alone.

Alone. She glanced around her bedroom. It had a cornflower blue carpet and delicate flowered paper in blue and white. Heavy white satin drapes were looped back from the window and matched the coverlet on the huge bed. King-size but only used by a queen. Smiling, she pulled the silk sheets around her. No amount of luxury could compensate for loneliness, but tonight it did not impinge on her with the same depressing degree. It had done her good to spend the day with Guy; she really must try to cultivate more friends.

In the morning she still had the same mild sense of contentment and, entering her office, felt able to cope with whatever problem the day might bring.

'Mr Smith has been asking to see you,' Mrs Maxwell said, putting a bundle of letters in front of her. 'There's nothing of importance in your correspondence, though you asked me to remind you to write to Busband Chemicals. You were going to make up your mind whether or not to accept their offer of a directorship.'

'I've decided against it,' Paula said. 'Their Board Meetings would bore me silly.'

'They do cosmetics,' said Mrs Maxwell. 'You might learn a few things.'

'That boot polish is used for mascara! I know that already!' Paula dropped her mink coat into her secretary's arms and sat down behind her desk. 'I'll see Ron Smith now.'

The interview with her editor was brief. Several of their biggest wholesalers had rung through to say there had been an unprecedented demand for the *Sunday Recorder* and they wanted to increase their orders for the following week. Without question the industrial espionage series was still pulling in the readers.

'What's lined up for next Sunday?' she asked.

'I'll still be concentrating on Rossiter. But the more personal stuff. His background and youth; the friends he had at school and university; his marriage and family relationships. Readers like to get a feel for the person they're reading about—it makes him more real.'

'You mean the better they know him the better they can enjoy his crucifixion!'

'That's a tough way of putting it.'

'We're in a tough business.'

'I'm glad you're backing me on this, Miss Grayson.'

'I'm backing the truth,' she said coolly.

He took the point. 'Every fact we've printed has been double-checked. I give you my word on that.'

'Good. If I——' She stopped as Mrs Maxwell came in. It was rare for her secretary to interrupt her during a meeting and she knew it must be important.

'Mr Gregory Scott is outside and wishes to see you.'

Paula could not hide her surprise. She recognised the name, having seen it frequently on law reports—and always on the winning side. Both Government and Opposition had asked him to stand for Parliament, but he had consistently refused, saying he did not wish to do anything that might conflict with his law practice. It was also rumoured that he had turned down several influential positions in public companies, and the last rumour, still making the rounds, was that he had been persuaded, by one of the biggest companies, to change his mind.

But that still didn't tell her why he was here. Had he come on behalf of clients to see if she was willing to sell her company or did he represent someone who had already made a bid? That he should arrive without an appointment indicated a matter of urgency and she was unwilling to refuse to see him.

'We'll finish our talk later,' she said to Ron Smith, and waited until he had left the room, using the door that led directly into the corridor, before telling Mrs Maxwell to show in her visitor.

Paula's first thought on seeing Gregory Scott was astonishment that he should be the man who had impinged so forcibly on her at the opera on Friday. Her second was to wish she had put on fresh powder and lipstick. But she dismissed both thoughts hastily and greeted him with a smile.

If he was aware that they had met before, he gave no sign of it, but strode forcefully across the silver-grey carpet.

'Good morning, Miss Grayson. I'm glad you've found time to see me without an appointment. It at least shows you're aware of the dangerous situation you're in.'

Not waiting to be told, he sat down opposite her. In daylight he was even more pugnacious-looking than she had remembered, though perhaps this came from the sharp tilt of his head and the thrusting position of his jaw. His eyes were so dark a brown that they appeared to merge with the pupils, increasing their brilliance and giving them a searchlight quality of penetration. Though he was conservatively dressed in a black pinstriped suit, it did not disguise the abrasiveness of his personality. His black hair had a slight wave and had obviously received a vigorous brushing to keep it in position, though a thick strand in the front refused to lie down and looked as if the slightest move of his head would make it rise like an angry coxcomb. That he was already angry was suddenly made clear to her by the way he slapped his hand down sharply on the briefcase on his lap, and spoke again.

'After my conversation with Mr Ardrey yesterday, I expected to have a full-scale retraction in your morning paper.'

Paula looked at him blankly. Had someone forgotten to tell her something important this morning or had he come to the wrong newspaper office?

'I'm afraid I don't follow you, Mr Scott. If you could explain. . . .'

'My client is Jack Rossiter. And after the way your scandal sheet tried to destroy him, I——' Her gasp stopped him momentarily. 'Didn't Ardrey tell you I called him? I'd have thought he'd have been on to you at once.'

'He was.' Paula kept her voice expressionless. 'But he didn't mention your name.' She tried not to show surprise that he was Rossiter's lawyer. She had not thought a man like Rossiter could afford such a high-powered representative. 'I knew someone had spoken to Mr Ardrey yesterday,' she continued, 'but I hadn't realised it was you.'

'Are you going to print an apology to my client?' he asked bluntly. 'Or do you first wish me to have a meeting with your lawyers to discuss compensation for libel?'

'There's no question of libel, Mr Scott. The editor of the *Recorder* is not the sort of man to print lies.'

'Show me the newspaperman who doesn't!'

'I'm not prepared to argue against your bias,' she said stiffly. 'I've taken a personal interest in this series and I know that everything we've printed is true.'

'Not about my client.'

'About everyone,' she asserted. 'I spoke to Mr Smith on Friday and he assured me every fact has been checked and can be backed by hard evidence.'

'Don't you know that evidence can be manufactured? Particularly by a paper like yours!'

'If you've come here to be insulting. . . .'

'You know why I've come here. What I want to know now is what you're going to do about it.'

'Nothing. I stand by what I've said. The *Recorder* printed the truth.'

'The *Recorder* wouldn't know the truth if it tripped over it!'

'You have a poor opinion of newspapers,' she said angrily.

'I have no opinion of them beyond the fact that most of them should be consigned to the dustbin! They do more harm than good.' His jaw thrust forward. 'My client demands an immediate printed retraction and substantial damages.'

'We have printed the truth,' Paula asserted. 'And we have also printed the facts. Naturally your client insists he is innocent. If he didn't, he would lose his job.'

'He'll lose it anyway, if he can't find out who framed him. I want to know the source of your editor's information.'

'No editor would tell you that. But I can assure you every fact was carefully checked.'

'I've already told you that facts can be misinterpreted,' Gregory Scott said with quiet force.

'There has been no interpretation or *mis*interpretation put on any of Mr Rossiter's actions,' she said coldly. 'The article merely reported what happened and left the readers to make up their own minds.'

'No one with a mind would read the *Recorder*!'

The crudeness of the insult inflamed her. 'In that case I'm surprised you're so concerned about the harm it will do your client.'

'Because lies travel—like gossip. That article of yours will be discussed by the directors of Weaver Brothers and they want my client to show them your apology.'

'We have nothing for which to apologise. We have given
the public the facts and if it inconveniences your client——'

'Inconveniences him! You're destroying him.'

'I'm sorry.' The words were inadequate and she knew it,
but she could not think what else to say with safety. 'I
don't think we have anything more to discuss, Mr Scott.
If your client wishes to take action I'm sure you'll be able
to advise him what to do.'

'You're putting up an excellent bluff, Miss Grayson.'

'I'm not bluffing. I believe in the integrity of my staff.'

'Then you're either an idealist or a fool!'

Twin spots of colour flagged her cheeks and she resisted the urge to jump to her feet. Instead she flung her
pen down on the desk. It spattered ink across a pristine
sheet of white blotter.

'I have nothing more to say to you, Mr Scott.'

'I'll have plenty to say to *you*. Before I'm finished you'll
regret every word you printed about Mr Rossiter. Each one
will cost you a thousand pounds!'

Without another word he strode across the room, opened
the door and closed it behind him.

Expecting to hear it slam, she was surprised when he
shut it quietly, and saw his control as yet one more sign
of his strength. What an uncompromising enemy he would
make; was going to make, she amended, for she knew she
had not heard the last of him.

Within moments of Gregory Scott's departure, Paula's
temper had cooled sufficiently for her to ask Ron Smith
and Guy to come immediately to her office.

'It's the sort of thing we must expect,' the editor said
after she had recounted her interview with the lawyer. 'And
the harder we hit Rossiter the louder Scott will cry for
him.'

'I suppose you *are* completely sure of your facts?' Guy
demanded.

'What do you take me for?' Ron Smith was angry and

showed it. 'Anyway, you checked them yourself last week.'

'I still had to take your word on many of the facts.'

'My word is as good as yours. Not as polished, maybe, but——'

'*Gentlemen—please!*' Paula waved her arm in a moderate gesture. 'If Mr Scott could hear us now, he'd be delighted. The least we can do is not to divide *ourselves*.'

Both men looked uncomfortable, though Guy recovered his equilibrium first, having lost less of it. Paula looked from him to Ron Smith. How different they were: the editor, with his sharp tongue and rasping manner, and Guy, tall and slim and always in command of himself, with fair hair and a clear skin that made him seem younger than the thirty-three she knew him to be. She could not imagine that even as a young man he had ever been at a disadvantage.

'What were your sources of information, Ron?' she asked and, seeing his small eyes grow smaller, said bluntly: 'For God's sake don't quote journalistic integrity to me! I'm the proprietor of the *Recorder* and I want an answer to my question.'

He gave a slight shrug. 'I have signed statements from several people in Rossiter's department at Weaver Brothers. Men who've worked with him for the last eight years.'

'All of them?'

'The three who count: his two assistants and his secretary. They've known about his activities for a couple of years.'

'Why did they keep quiet?'

'It's a British habit to look the other way. Part of it was old school tie loyalty.'

'What school did the secretary go to?' Paula asked dryly.

'The school of love,' said Ron Smith, equally dryly. 'She's been hot for Rossiter for years. He's been a widower for more than ten and she had hopes of becoming the second wife. When she finally realised he didn't feel the same....'

Paula leaned back in her chair and looked at Guy, who nodded imperceptibly. 'Very well, Ron,' she said. 'I won't keep you any longer.'

'You will keep me in the picture, though?'

'Naturally.'

From the doorway he looked back at her. 'I print the truth, Miss Grayson. You own the *Recorder*, but it's mine too, and I'm going to make it the best Sunday paper in the country.'

'That's why you're its editor,' she said quietly, and gave him a faint smile as he went out.

Alone with Guy she allowed her disquiet to show. 'I know a hard-hitting series can build up sales, but I wish there were other ways of doing it. I hate destroying people.'

'It looks as if Rossiter destroyed himself. Smith made quite sure of his proof before he printed a single word.' Guy came round the side of the desk and put his hand on her shoulder. 'Have faith in him, Paula. You chose him for the job.'

'I know. It's just that he's young, and when you *are*, you're inclined to be over-enthusiastic. He might cut corners and——'

'I'm here to see he doesn't.' Guy's grip grew firmer. 'You've let Scott upset you—and that's playing right into his hands.'

'You think so?'

'I know so. He wants to make you doubt Ron Smith's integrity. Then he'll attack you again and hope you'll agree to print a retraction.'

'You sound very sure of his plans.'

'It's what I'd do if I were in his shoes.'

She tried and failed to see Guy as the pugnacious lawyer who had strode into her room half an hour earlier.

'I'm silly to let him upset me,' she apologised, 'but it's

the first time anything like this has happened since Father died. He always used to deal with these sort of problems.'

'Then leave *me* to deal with this one. I'll watch over Ron Smith as if I'm his mother! Stop worrying, Paula. I've seen the evidence and I assure you Rossiter is guilty.'

'What do you think will happen to him?'

'He'll probably go and work for the rival company.'

'That would be an admission of guilt.'

'What does he care? He's laughing all the way to the bank.'

'Couldn't Weaver Brothers sue him?'

'I'm sure they'd prefer to forget the whole thing. Anyway, they've probably done the same sort of skulduggery themselves. You should read the articles you publish,' he added with a slight smile. 'They've even taught *me* a few things about the way big business is run!'

'I have read them,' she said. 'But they didn't impinge on me until this morning.'

She thought over these words again when she was alone, and acknowledged that it was more than the articles which had impinged on her. It was her meeting with Gregory Scott. She could not remember ever being so aware of a man.

'He's not even good-looking,' she said aloud, 'unless you happen to like men who look like aggressive bulldogs.'

In this she knew she was doing him less than justice, but she was in no mood to be reasonable, and for the rest of the day felt irritable and on edge.

A Board Meeting kept her late at the office, after which she dined at the Savoy with Charles Edwards, a director of the Group and one of their senior auditors. It was after eleven o'clock when he drove her home, by which time her head was swimming with figures and budgets.

'You have an excellent grasp of things,' he murmured as he bade her goodnight. 'You're your father all over again.'

'I miss him very much.' The words came out before she

had realised they were in her mind. It showed her she was more disturbed by the morning's events than she had realised. And by the man who had caused them. Quickly she tried to forget him.

'Do you think I'm silly to carry on alone, Charles?'

'Are you referring to Grayson Publications or to Paula Grayson?' he asked with a slight smile.

'You do at least still see me as a woman,' she said, and hearing the faint bitterness in her voice, was sorry she had asked the question.

'Of course I see you as a woman. And an exceptional one—in every way. Which brings me back to *your* question and also to mine. On the face of it, you seem to be cut out for business, but——'

'I was never given a chance to do anything else. When other children were playing with toys, I was given copies of the *Recorder* and the *Daily News*! No matter what I'd wanted to do, Father would have expected me to take over from him.'

'You always acted as if it were what you wanted.'

'Acted,' she echoed. 'I'm not sure if I acted a part to please Father or if I genuinely wanted the role. Maybe I'll never know. It's become second nature to me now.'

'You could always sell out. You'd be an extremely wealthy woman.'

'And an extremely bored one. No, Charles, I'm too used to the harness to discard it!'

'Then share the load, either in your business life or your personal one. A good husband would be ideal.'

'But where is the ideal husband?' she queried.

'If I were twenty years younger, he'd be standing right next to you!'

She laughed and kissed him on the cheek. 'I feel better already, Charles. Who needs a husband when I can talk to you?'

'Young women need more than talk.' Charles Edwards

stepped back to survey her. 'Marriage, Paula. Think about
it.'

'Men don't like women who have power. They want it
for themselves.'

'So find someone who understands the business and
share it with him.'

Implicit in this advice was the suggestion that she turn
to Guy. Charles was too tactful to put it more clearly than
he had already done, and she was too tactful to say she had
already thought about the idea and discarded it.

'I'll bear in mind what you've said,' she promised, and
entering the house, straight away put it from her mind.

To marry Guy, or any other man who could share her
work load and responsibility, would only serve to bring
her business life directly into her private one. And she had
had enough of that with her father. Unless she could love
—and be loved—by a man who saw her primarily as his
wife and mother of his children, she wanted no part of marriage.

CHAPTER FOUR

THE fretfulness which Paula took to bed with her accom-
panied her to the office next day, and she was irritable with
her editors at the morning conference and edgy with her
secretary.

'Is there anything worrying you, Miss Grayson?' Mrs
Maxwell asked, when Paula made an unusually sharp comment to her.

'Nothing whatever,' Paula said shortly, and proceeded
to disprove it by dealing with all her correspondence in an
unusually staccato manner.

It was only as she looked up from dictating a terse

memorandum to be sent to all the journalists who sub-
mitted monthly expense accounts, and saw her secretary's
long-suffering expression, that her ill-humour vanished and
she chuckled.

'You'd better scrap that memo, Mrs Maxwell. I think
it will be wiser if I leave things as they are.'

'I knew you would.'

'Why? Because of my better nature?'

'Because you're so like your father. Whenever he was in
a temper about something, he'd have a blitz on the waste
of office stationery. For days afterwards we'd count every
sheet of paper. When *you're* upset you go for expense
accounts!'

'They're equally impossible to curtail!' Paula gave a wry
smile. 'You have me well taped, Mrs Maxwell. I suppose
you'll be telling me next you know what caused my mood?'

'Mr Scott,' came the swift answer. 'He could upset anyone.' The woman rose, notebook in hand. 'I'll start on these
letters, Miss Grayson, unless there's anything else you
want to dictate?'

Paula shook her head and Mrs Maxwell went out. Within
a moment she returned carrying a graceful white vase
filled with freesias. There must have been at least twenty
dozen crammed together in a riot of delicate colours, their
scent filling the air with a heady fragrance that reminded
Paula of spring.

'How gorgeous!' she exclaimed, and wondered who
could have sent them to her. Christmas and the New Year
brought countless bouquets and bottles of scent, but it was
rare for her to receive anything at any other time, unless she
was indisposed and away from the office.

'A note came with it.' Mrs Maxwell handed her an
envelope.

Paula opened it and looked at the small, heavily pres-
sured writing on the card. Her heart gave an extraordinary
leap and then started to race.

'It's from Mr Scott,' she said casually, and pointed to a table on the far side of the room. 'Put the flowers there.'

'Wouldn't you prefer them on your desk? Then you could smell them.'

'There're so many, I'd be able to smell them if they were in the corridor. Put them on the table.'

Mrs Maxwell did as she was told and left the room. Only then did Paula look at the card again and read the message.

Forgive me—Gregory Scott.

It was the succinct type of apology she would have expected from him had she been expecting any apology at all. It was also capable of two interpretations, and she wondered which one he meant. Was he asking forgiveness for losing his temper with her or for accusing one of her newspapers of lying about his client?

'Mr Scott is on the line for you.' Mrs Maxwell's voice came over the intercom.

Paula reached for the receiver and then stopped. 'Keep him holding for a couple of minutes and then put him through.'

She leaned back in her chair and tried to still the tremors that were coursing through her body. It was crazy to let herself be so aware of his man. She drew several deep breaths and then picked up the telephone.

'Paula Grayson speaking,' she said.

'Do you?' Gregory Scott asked, his voice deep and incisive.

'Do I what?'

'Forgive me?'

She glanced across at the flowers, a rainbow of colours against the silver-grey wall. 'Such beautiful flowers beg forgiveness, Mr Scott. But there was no need for them.'

'I think there was.'

'No,' she reiterated. 'I am a newspaper proprietor and used to people losing their temper with me.'

'It wasn't the newspaper proprietor with whom I was

losing my temper.' If anything, his voice became deeper. 'It was with Paula Grayson. That's why I sent you the flowers.'

'What did you have against Paula Grayson?' she asked in surprise.

'The fact that she could make me so aware of her that I lost my control—and with it my temper. I assure you I'm renowned for my icy calm.'

'Really?' She could not keep the amusement from her voice. 'I find that hard to believe. On both the occasions I've seen you, I thought you extremely short-tempered.'

'So you did remember!'

Her hand trembled on the telephone. He had remembered too, yet how skilfully he had hidden it yesterday when he had come to her office.

'Of course,' she said. 'I don't forget people I tread on.'

'That remark could be taken two ways!'

Her laugh this time was spontaneous and he echoed it. As it died away she spoke again.

'Thank you once more for the flowers, Mr Scott. It was——'

'Are you free to have dinner with me tonight?'

She was so surprised by the invitation that she could not think what to say.

'I can collect you at eight or eight-thirty,' he went on. 'Or later still, if you prefer it.'

Only then did she find her voice, and with it came anger.

'It won't do your client any good for you to have dinner with me, Mr Scott.'

'My client isn't asking you to have dinner with him, Miss Grayson. *I* am.' Gregory Scott's voice was as cool as her own. 'And I try to leave business behind me when I leave the office.'

'I don't——'

'I'd like to see you,' he cut in. 'Besides, it will give you a chance to tread on my other foot!'

His humour put her at a disadvantage, making her feel
she was on the defensive for no good cause. Why shouldn't
she accept his invitation? She was not doing anything else
tonight and it could make for an interesting evening.

'Call for me at eight,' she said. 'Thirty-four Hamilton
Grove.'

'Good.'

The telephone clicked and she was left holding a dead
receiver. Usually she was the one who did this, and the
knowledge was wry. She put the receiver back on its
cradle and smiled. The abrupt way Gregory Scott had
hung up was typical of the man. He had got what he
wanted and saw no point in continuing the conversation.
She pushed back her chair and went over to the table. The
scent of the freesias was far stronger here. Mrs Maxwell was
right—it was silly to leave them at this end of the room.
Carefully she lifted the bowl and transferred it to her desk.

That evening she changed twice before being satisfied
with her appearance, discarding a long-sleeved black crêpe
—which she thought made her look too businesslike—for
one of similar style but in velvet. It was amazing how the
different textured material altered the appearance of the
dress. The velvet gave her skin a pearly lustre which, in
turn, emphasised the honey-coloured lights in the heavy
fall of tawny hair that swung forward across one cheek.
Excitement made her eyes glow like topaz and she deliberately refrained from emphasising them by mascara, unwilling for her escort to think she had gone to any trouble
over her appearance. Because of this she wore no jewellery
either. She would let black velvet and sable speak for her.

At eight o'clock she was waiting in the drawing-room,
sipping a glass of champagne and glancing through one of
the evening papers. At ten past eight she thought Gregory
Scott was not going to come and at quarter past was convinced of it. She stood up and, as she did so, heard the
butler cross the hall to the front door. With trembling

fingers she held on to her glass, though she looked serene as the drawing-room door opened and Gregory Scott walked in. He was exactly as she had first remembered him: suave in a dinner jacket, its stark black and white emphasising his crisp looks and manner.

'Traffic,' he said succinctly. 'I didn't want to arrive early, so I parked for a while in Regents Park and then got caught in a snarl-up.'

'Where were you coming from?'

'Home. I have an apartment in St James'.'

'I suppose it's more convenient than a house.' She knew she was making unnecessary conversation but could not help it.

'I have a place in the country too,' he said.

'I can't see you in tweeds. Do you mow the lawn and take the dog for a walk?'

'Dogs,' he corrected. 'I have two red setters. No ferret and no bulldog!'

Her eyes widened and his own crinkled at the corners as he smiled. 'I've been likened to both breeds before now. The pugnacity of a bulldog and the determination of a ferret!'

She laughed and moved to the sideboard.

'Champagne would be delightful,' he said as she indicated the bottle.

She poured a glass and handed it to him. 'Don't you mind what people say about you, Mr Scott?'

'If everyone started to *like* me, I would mind very much. I made my name in litigation and the more successful one is, the more enemies one makes.'

Watching him cross the room to the mantelpiece and look at the Bonnard, she could not envisage him being perturbed by what anyone thought of him. He exuded the rare quality of total unconcern, as if he were so sure of himself that he had no need of other people's liking. I bet he never even looks in a mirror except to shave. The thought made her smile and, as he turned to face her, he saw it.

'What have I said to amuse you, Miss Grayson?'

'How do you know I was thinking of you?'

'Masculine intuition!' He came a step closer. 'You are as aware of me as I am of you. It happened the moment we met. If anyone had told me it could, I would have laughed them out of court.'

'I don't know what you're talking about.'

'Awareness,' he replied. 'Empathy—sexual attraction. Call it what you will, it all boils down to the same thing: two people meet and they know instantly that they could be important to each other.'

'Your line is not very original, Mr Scott,' she said dryly, turning to replenish her glass. 'Many men have told me I can be important to them.'

He chuckled. 'I'm glad you're witty.'

'Didn't your awareness tell you that I was?'

'It's told me many things. But I'm not sure how far I can trust it. As I said, it's never happened to me before.' He came to her side. 'I've booked a table at the Capital. I won't ask if you've been there before. That's one of the disadvantages of taking out a beautiful and important woman. One can never surprise her.'

'I'm sure you could find a way!'

'I'd like to think so,' he agreed, and set down his glass. 'I'm ready to leave when you are.'

His car was parked outside the house. It was black and low-slung and she did not recognise the make though she guessed it was foreign. The chauffeur at the wheel surprised her, for she had expected him to drive himself.

'I only drive in the country,' he said, divining her thoughts with alarming ability. 'When I'm working I concentrate so much that I'm apt to drive without thought.'

'So seeing me tonight is part of your work?' she questioned ironically.

'Perhaps it's my life's work,' he said so quickly that she laughed.

'*Your* wit isn't bad either, Mr Scott.'

'I must display it as often as I can. I like to hear you laugh. It's uninhibited yet shy.'

'I don't see how the two go together.'

'The rarity makes it all the more charming. You have the uninhibitedness that comes with being successful, plus the shyness of a girl.'

The compliment struck her as being forced and she was irritated by it. 'I'm twenty-seven, Mr Scott. I can hardly be considered a girl.'

'You look far younger,' he commented.

'You must surely know I'm not. One of the penalties of success is that everyone knows everything about you.'

'I know nothing about you.' He half turned, the better to look at her. 'I hope you'll tell me.'

'I'll send you a biography.'

'I'd rather hear it from you.'

'I don't like talking about myself,' she prevaricated.

'I must try to make you change your mind.'

During dinner, he was as good as his word, plying her with excellent food, wine and charm in equal proportions. Not until the meal was over and they were sipping coffee did Paula realise how adroitly he had extracted information from her about her childhood and youth. It was a disconcerting discovery and put her on her guard.

'Do you always subject your guests to a catechism?' she asked.

'Only those I'm curious about.' He eyed her frankly. 'And I'm extremely curious about you.'

She shrugged but said nothing and he went on eyeing her.

'You can catechise *me* if you like. I have no secrets.'

'I don't believe that for a start.'

He chuckled. It was a deep-throated sound and she was fascinated at the way his looks changed when he relaxed.

Yet he still exuded the same air of command. His black brows had the same incisive line above his eyes and the wide mouth was still firmly controlled. Here was a man one should never take lightly.

'Did you always want to be a lawyer?' she asked.

'Ever since I can remember.'

'Why?'

'Because I enjoy giving advice and getting people out of tight corners. Law seemed the best way of doing it.'

'Do you still feel the same?'

'Not quite. I've widened my scope in the past few years. My clients no longer wait till they're in trouble before coming to see me. They now ask me for advice *before* they do anything—instead of after! It means I'm not only concerned with their legal affairs but with their business ones as well.'

'So you're not just a litigious lawyer?' she smiled.

'Not primarily. I'm more of a business counsellor. In fact I hardly have time to practise law these days.'

'How modest you are!'

'I'm giving you the facts,' he said crisply. 'Interpret them the way you will.'

'How do I interpret your asking me to have dinner with you tonight?'

'As a personal indulgence. Though you obviously find that hard to believe.'

Her shoulders lifted slightly. 'Like you, I'm a realist. I find it impossible to ignore the facts.'

'Which are?'

'That I own the *Sunday Recorder*. I'm truly sorry I can't help you—but I never interfere in editorial policy unless I'm planning to fire the editor.'

'Are you telling me that nothing I say or do will make you alter the series or keep my client's name out of it?'

She forced herself to meet his gaze. 'Yes, Mr Scott, that's exactly what I'm telling you.'

'Thank God for that! Now maybe you'll believe I'm seeing you for personal reasons only.' He leaned across the table and put his hand on her arm. 'You're a beautiful and intelligent woman, Paula Grayson. I can see you aren't used to using your beauty, but I assumed you had long practice in using your intelligence!'

There was both compliment and jibe in his remark, and she was torn between chagrin and pleasure.

'I don't use the fact that I'm a woman to get me what I want,' she stated. 'If that's what you meant by the first part of your comment——'

'You know it wasn't. I was referring to your innocence.'

'My innocence?'

He nodded. 'As far as business is concerned, you're wide awake. But in your personal life, you're still asleep!'

'Waiting for Prince Charming, no doubt?'

'Exactly.'

'I hope I'll wake up when he arrives.'

'I'll make sure you do.'

She drew back in her chair. Did he know what he had said or had he been carried away by his own rhetoric? She lowered her eyes from his, and only then became aware of his hand on her arm. His fingers were strong and tanned against the paleness of her skin; his wrists twice as broad as her own, with soft black hairs on them, curling against the crisp whiteness of his cuff. The sheer animal strength of him began to affect her and she could almost believe she was experiencing the empathy he had referred to earlier.

'I had to see you again, Paula,' he said softly. 'And I want to go on seeing you. Paula,' he repeated her name, lingering on it as though he enjoyed saying it. 'It suits you. It's masculine and feminine.'

'My father had hoped for a son,' she said baldly. 'He was going to call him Paul.'

'And you were second best?'

'Yes.'

'He didn't think it when he died.'

'How do you know?'

'He wouldn't have left you his entire empire.'

Gregory Scott leaned back in his chair and lit a cheroot. It suited his character better than a cigar and she liked the smell of the pungent tobacco.

'I made it my business to find out about you,' he continued. 'You worked with your father from the time you left school and he always treated you as his heir.'

'Without favouritism, Mr Scott.'

'Almost on too tight a rein,' he conceded. 'Your self-control is frightening.'

'It's second nature,' she shrugged.

'Do you always say and do the right thing?'

'I always try to behave normally.'

'Do you know what normal is? I have the feeling you've never had a chance to be normal. All your life you have been what your father wanted you to be.'

These were words Paula had not dared say to herself and she found it impossible to let someone else say them. They awoke too many dormant fears; made substance out of much which she still wanted to deny.

'It's past midnight, Mr Scott. I would like to go home.'

Outside the hotel he glanced swiftly up and down the road before leading her northwards.

'Oates has parked the car somewhere along here. I told him I'd drive myself home.'

'You mean you aren't concentrating on business any more?'

Even in the darkness she saw his smile as he bent to unlock the car and help her in. He drove with much less verve than she had expected, keeping well within the speed limit and not bothering to overtake.

'When may I see you again?' he asked suddenly.

'I'm not sure when I'm free.'

'Don't you like me?'

'I don't know you,' she shrugged.

'I'm trying to remedy that. Are you free tomorrow?'

'No.'

'Thursday?'

'I'm afraid not.'

'Friday, then?'

'Don't you go to the country for the weekend?'

'I'm prepared to stay in town if you'll see me.'

'Please don't,' she said quickly. 'It's a waste of your time.'

'Why can't you see me tomorrow?' he insisted.

'I'm having dinner with one of my directors.'

'Leave him early and I'll take you dancing.'

'Dancing!'

Her amazement made him laugh. 'Don't you like dancing?'

'I don't know. It's a long time since I've been.'

'Your men friends must be very remiss,' he commented.

'My men friends are not dancing types!'

'They don't know what they're missing. I bet *you're* a good dancer.'

'I used to be,' she admitted.

'I'm sure you still are. It's like riding a bicycle—once you can, you never forget it. Come on, Paula, live dangerously! Tell me where I can collect you tomorrow night.'

Envisaging the gossip that would rage if Gregory Scott picked her up from the Press Club, she shook her head.

'I'm not sure what time I'll be free. It will be better if I can meet you as soon as I'm able to get away.'

'The Star Roof, then. Do you know it?'

'I've heard of it.' She drew a deep breath. 'I'll see you there about eleven.'

The car slowed down and with surprise she saw they were driving along Hamilton Grove.

'Would you like to come in for a drink?' she asked as they stopped outside her discreetly lighted front door.

'So much that I think it's best for me to refuse.'

He walked with her up the steps and drew her hand to his lips. 'Goodnight, lovely Paula—until tomorrow.'

Without a backward glance he returned to his car, but did not start it until he saw her go into the hall and close the door.

She waited until he had driven away before going up to her room, trying to tell herself that this evening was no different from any of the others she had spent dining with a man. But she knew this was not true. There was a world of difference, and no matter what happened, Gregory Scott was not someone she would easily forget; even if she wanted to do so.

CHAPTER FIVE

IT was not until six o'clock the following evening that Paula finally committed herself to going dancing with Gregory.

Twice she had almost rung him to say she could not meet him, but each time she had stopped herself from doing so by the belief that he would see her refusal as a fear of meeting him again. And how right he would be! So right that she refused to give him the chance of finding out.

She deliberately wore black again: a starkly plain dress that covered her from head to toe. She was giving him no chance to find her feminine or ethereal. Her hair style was sophisticated too, swept back from her face and curved into an austere French pleat. Solitaire diamonds sparkled on her lobes and a large, matching ring glowed like white fire on her finger.

It was eleven-fifteen before her dinner engagement came to an end. Her host had insisted she dismiss her chauffeur and he drove her home himself, hovering on the doorstep and looking so willing to come in that she felt guilty for not asking him. But pleading a headache—woman's time-honoured excuse—she bade him goodnight and left him.

Hovering in the marble-floored hall she was overcome with shame at her behaviour; not for the way she had just acted—she felt no guilt for not prolonging the evening—but for her desire to spend the rest of it with Gregory Scott. How amused he would be to know he was causing her to behave like an excited schoolgirl suffering the pangs of first love!

Once again she debated whether to send him a message saying she could not get away, and she was still undecided when Frederick, her father's chauffeur and now hers, came through from the kitchen quarters to say that the car was at the door.

'There was no need for you to stay on duty,' she protested. 'I could easily have taken a taxi.'

'I would have been waiting for you at the Press Club if Mr Chalmers hadn't asked you to send me home,' he replied. 'So all I did was to wait here instead. More comfortable too,' he added. 'There was a good documentary on B.B.C.2.'

'You should have gone home,' she said.

'And miss out on my overtime?'

He opened the front door and she followed him to the car, knowing he had got the best of the argument.

'You're always telling me that income tax doesn't make it worth your while to do any overtime,' she commented, still not willing to concede defeat.

'Every little helps, Miss Grayson.'

'You're incorrigible, Fred. It's time you stopped pampering me.'

'It's become a habit.'

She settled back in the seat and watched the lamp-posts flash by. There was little traffic about at this hour and they reached Knightsbridge in less than ten minutes.

As they drew up outside the discreetly lit entrance of the club, her regret at coming here was so strong that she leaned forward to tell her chauffeur to drive on. But before she could say a word, the door was abruptly opened and Gregory Scott appeared.

'I'm not letting you turn tail and run,' he said by way of greeting.

She caught her breath on a gasp. 'Masculine intuition again?'

'I need it to keep a step ahead of you.'

He led her across the carpeted entrance to a small lift. They seemed to go up for a long way before emerging into a glass-walled bar that gave them a magnificent view of London. Beyond the bar lay the night club, large and dimly lit; full of people yet appearing secluded because each table was screened by eye-level banks of greenery.

'It looks a bit like a jungle,' she remarked, trying to keep the conversation light as they were led to a corner table.

'It goes well with my mood,' he smiled.

Deeming it wiser not to comment, she pretended to a great interest in the dancing couples and, without a word, Gregory rose again and held out his hand.

She followed him on to the floor, her body tense as his arms came around her. His clasp was light, almost pressureless, and he danced with unexpected fluidity. He made no attempt to hold her close and she felt a momentary sense of disappointment. After several moments he led her back to the table where champagne and sandwiches were awaiting them.

'I don't know about you,' he said, 'but I'm starving.'

'Didn't you have dinner?' she asked.

'I was working in my office until half an hour ago.'

'You love your work.' She made it a statement and he nodded.

'It's my hobby as well as my profession.'

He poured champagne for them both and then tucked into the sandwiches. The gusto with which he ate amused her and also gave her an unexpected tenderness towards him. It was easy to imagine what he had been like as a little boy: serious and determined; naughty too, but always honest about it.

'Do you have any brothers and sisters?' she asked curiously.

'My brother is a surgeon.' He smiled. 'And I know what you're going to say to that! He cuts people up on the table and I cut them up in court!'

She smiled. 'English lawyers can't go into court.'

'That's why the barristers who represent my clients are only chosen on the basis of their doing what I tell them!'

She flung back her head and laughed, only stopping as she saw he was watching her with darkening eyes.

'Why are you looking at me like that?' she asked.

'Like what?'

'As if you ... as if you——'

'Want to kiss you? Because I do.'

'Don't say that!' she protested.

'Why not? It's true.'

He stood up and once again led her on to the floor. This time his hands were less gentle as he pulled her close. The warmness of his body seeped through her dress and his chest was hard against the softness of her breasts. It was impossible not to be aware of him and though she tried to hold herself aloof, the steady beat of the music infiltrated her senses. He rested his cheek against hers and she made no protest; nor did she say anything when his lips touched the curve of her ear.

'Darling Paula,' he murmured.

She waited, half expecting him to say more, but he didn't, and she knew he was too canny to commit himself in words. She tried to draw away from him, but he felt the movement and gripped her more tightly.

'Oh no, you don't,' he said. 'I've got you close and that's the way you're going to remain.'

'Are you as determined with all your women friends?'

'Yes.'

This was not the answer she wanted and she was annoyed with herself for feeling annoyed. 'I suppose you have quite a few?'

'Not at the same time.' He gave her a slight shake. 'I'm a big boy, Paula. These days, no red-blooded man need pine for want of a woman.'

'I'll bet!'

'It applies equally to women.'

'Yes.'

They danced in silence.

'Care to add to that?' he asked.

'No.'

He chuckled. 'You're a cool customer, my dear, but you don't fool me. You're a kitten in tigerish clothes!'

'And you're ready to show me how to grow up?'

'I'd never say anything as trite as that. You're far too intelligent to be wooed by the mediocre.'

'And you're planning to woo me?'

'Of course.' His tongue gently caressed the lobe of her ear and she turned her head sharply.

'Don't do that!'

Instantly he stopped. 'You're right. There's a time and place for everything.'

'Not for us, Mr Scott. I don't like flirting.'

'That makes two of us,' he retorted, and twirled her round until she was breathless, before leading her back to their table.

They remained at the night club till well after two, and it was only when he saw her stifle a yawn that he suggested they leave. Paula could not remember the last time she had returned home so late, and she said so as he put the key in the lock of her front door and opened it.

'You've missed out on a lot of fun,' was his reply, and he bent and kissed the tip of her nose. Then he drew away and looked into her eyes. He was only a little taller than she was, yet so powerfully built that he seemed to loom above her.

'Are you free to see me over the weekend if I stay in town?' he asked.

She hesitated, longing to say yes but reluctant to give in.

'I'll stay,' he said without waiting for her reply and, as he had done the night before, went quickly to his car and drove off without a backward glance.

Expecting to feel irritated by his high-handed behaviour, Paula could only feel rather pleased, and she closed the door and went up to her room. She was behaving like a schoolgirl instead of a woman of the world; and certainly not in the way anyone would expect Paula Grayson to act. The vague depression she had felt with her life returned with renewed vigour and its cause could no longer be denied. She was tired of living alone; dispirited at having to cope with problems all day and return to a solitary house at night. This was the root cause of her dissatisfaction.

The solution was to marry Guy. Yet it was foolish to accept one man simply because she was in danger of falling in love with another. The thought caught her unawares and she stood by the bed, caught in a mindless panic. Why was she allowing Gregory Scott to fill her mind like this? She hardly knew him. And she definitely did not trust him. Yet when he had held her in his arms on the dance floor. . . .

'So I wanted him,' she said aloud. 'But that has nothing to do with love.'

The matter-of-fact assertion conquered her fear. Why shouldn't she be attracted to him? He was a handsome brute and she had reached the stage where male assertion seemed particularly attractive. If only Guy had a stronger personality! Didn't he realise that the only way he could get her to marry him was to insist they do it? To order her and not to ask? If Gregory Scott wanted to marry a woman he wouldn't waste his time trying to cajole her into it. He'd carry her off like the caveman he was!

She took off her earrings and set them on the dressing-table. The mirror reflected her movement and she stared at herself. Tall, aloof, soignée. Quite different from the steamy hot thoughts that were projecting even steamier pictures in front of her.

Abruptly she turned away from the mirror. She was not going to see Gregory again. She would drop him a note tomorrow and tell him.

With her breakfast tray the next morning there arrived a bouquet of flowers so vast that her maid, Janet, could hardly stagger into the bedroom with it.

'They came at seven o'clock this morning,' the girl said. 'Delivered in a taxi straight from Covent Garden.'

Paula picked up the envelope nestling among the blooms: freesias again and dozens of tulips and irises.

'Put them in water for me,' she ordered, and only when the maid went in seach of vases did she look at the card.

'Don't drop me a note to say you can't see me this week-end,' Gregory wrote, 'because I won't believe you. I'm staying in town and I intend to spend Saturday and Sunday with you.'

She flung the card on to the eiderdown. Damn the man—was he psychic too? Angrily she banged the top of her egg. Yolk spurted on to the napkin and she glared at it. Then suddenly she laughed. Picking up the card again, she re-read it. Very well, Mr oh-so-confident Scott, if you want to flirt with me, then two can play at the same game. But it won't do your client a bit of good. I can promise you that.

For the next few days Paula kept herself fully occupied with work. But Gregory Scott was in her thoughts more frequently than she liked and several times she toyed with the idea of writing to say she had to go out of town on business and could not see him at the weekend. Because he had tried to cut off her retreat there was no reason for her not to retreat; indeed if she didn't, she would be playing right into his hands. She was still undecided what to do when Ron Smith brought her the proofs of the article that would appear in Sunday's *Recorder*. She read it carefully. It was as hard-hitting as the previous one and knocked several more nails in the coffin of Jack Rossiter.

'Have we had any comeback from what we printed last week?' she asked.

'A visit from John Moreham. He's a director of Weaver Brothers. He saw Mr Ardrey yesterday—I thought he'd have told you.'

She shook her head and made a note on her pad to call Guy. She did so as soon as Ron Smith had gone, cutting short his explanation by asking him to come to her office at once. She so rarely made an order sound like one—she was still woman enough to know how much men resented this—that he came up with astonishing speed, full of apologies and explanations.

'I was going to tell you, of course, but not until I'd got it sorted out. I didn't want to worry you with it.'

'I'm in the worry business,' she said testily. 'When I need protection, I'll hire a guard. Now tell me what he said.'

'It had nothing to do with Rossiter.'

'Really?' She was amazed.

'In fact he only mentioned him in passing. What he wanted from us was sight of all the other information we have about any of their employees.'

'What a nerve!'

'That's what I thought. I told him our series deals with industrial espionage as a whole, not as a clean-up campaign of Weaver Brothers staff.'

'I bet that pleased him.'

Guy smiled. 'He went out of his way to tell me they

own a large block of shares in our company.'

'Oh, do they?' Paula retorted, and was reaching for the telephone when Guy stopped her.

'I've already spoken to our brokers. They don't own enough to bother us.'

She looked at him gratefully. 'You think of everything. I don't know what I'd do without you.'

'Find someone else.' He looked rueful. 'The last few weeks you've been so distant with me that I've rather wondered if you *had*.'

'Don't be silly. It's just that I've been busy. Whenever audit time comes round, I get inundated, you should know that by now.'

He looked unconvinced by her explanation, but did not put it into words. 'I'm going to Sussex to see Mother on Saturday. If you're free to come with me, I know she'd be delighted to see you.'

'Not this weekend, Guy, I'm tied up.'

As always he accepted her refusal with grace and she watched him go with unusual exasperation. If he took no for an answer so easily, he would only have himself to blame if she.... She stopped the rest of the thought by pressing the buzzer sharply for Mrs Maxwell.

Driving home from the office on Friday evening, Paula decided to have an early night. Apart from the flowers and the note there had been no further word from Gregory Scott, but she was convinced he had given careful thought to the coming weekend. It was going to be the apex of his softening-up process of her. He would be at his most charming and magnetic. She smiled as she thought of the dresses she had bought with this in mind. The hunter hunted! The victim becoming the victor! But he would find out too late.

On and off during the evening, Paula savoured the seduction she had planned, and could not make up her mind whether to get it over with on Saturday or to string it out until Sunday. She decided finally to wait until Sunday, when Gregory had read the latest article in the *Recorder*. That was when he would make his plea for Jack Rossiter and that was when she would deliver her *coup de grâce* and fling down the proofs of the article Ron Smith had already written for the following Sunday. An article that would make it impossible for Rossiter to deny his guilt, for it included a photograph of a cheque made out to him from a director of Daybright. Let Gregory Scott put that in his briefcase and take it to court!

During the evening she half expected him to call her, and each time the telephone rang she tensed. But there was no word from him until Saturday morning at ten, when she was taking a leisurely bath.

'I hope I haven't woken you,' he asked without sounding in the least apologetic.

'I'm in the bath.'

There was a pause. 'I'm not going to make the obvious remark.'

'You already have!'

'Clever girl. Now hunt the soap and tell me how long it will take you to be ready.'

She smiled at the receiver, glad he could not see it. 'I didn't think I'd be seeing you till this evening,' she said archly.

'And waste the whole day? Oh no, my dear, we've a busy schedule ahead of us. I'll collect you in an hour. Put on your walking shoes and something warm.'

'Where are we going?'

'Out,' he said, and left her with the dialling tone ringing in her ear.

Carefully Paula prepared herself for Gregory Scott and the weather. The amber gold cashmere dress was for the man, the fur jacket and brogues for the cold February day. Her thick, tawny brown hair was almost hidden by a white fox cap, which matched the muff that encased her hands.

This part of her oufit was definitely gilt on the lily. The man wasn't yet born who could resist a young woman in white fur!

Gregory Scott arrived in a small sports car. It was black, like his limousine, but the interior was scarlet and opulent, as was the thick rug which he wrapped around her as she sat beside him.

'Sensible shoes?' he said, glancing at her feet. 'I'm glad you took my advice.'

'I'll be furious if we end up lunching at the Ritz!'

'No fear of that,' he assured her.

'Where are we going?'

'Wait and see.'

He set the car in motion and seemed content not to talk. Paula was glad of the silence, for she found his proximity disturbing. Today he looked exceedingly carefree. His hair was ruffled by the breeze that blew in through the window that he kept open on his side, though he had first solicitously made sure it would not be too cold for her. He wore heavy cavalry twill trousers that hugged the lean line of his thigh and calf, and a thick white sweater that exaggerated the glow of his skin, making it look swarthy instead of pale. His hair looked very black too, against the white wool, and she noticed he wore it so long on his neck that the ends curled against the collar and around the sides of his ears. He was staring intently at the road and whistling tunelessly through his teeth, his mouth pursed forward, which made his jawline more thrusting than ever.

As if aware of her scrutiny, he glanced at her. His eyes were bright and shiny as a bird's—a warm brown this morning—fringed by their thick black lashes.

'Do tell me where we're going,' she pleaded. 'Then I'll be able to anticipate it.'

'Southend,' he said, and laughed at her astonishment. He pressed his foot harder on the accelerator. Hedgerows leaped past and the studs on the road thudded beneath their wheels.

'I'll wager you've never eaten cockles and whelks,' he shouted above the roar of the engine.

'That's the only thing missing from my life!'

'Not for much longer. You'll be hungry by the time we get to the sea.'

Paula thought of the breakfast she had been too tense to eat and felt hungry already—but not for whelks. A nice plate of bacon and eggs was more in her line. She curled down in the seat and bit back a chuckle. Inexplicably she knew she was going to enjoy today.

It was a tired and replete Paula who returned to Hamilton Grove at five-thirty that evening. Gregory had been an entertaining companion and the hours had flown by.

Together they had eaten a huge breakfast at a small Italian restaurant on the sea front, then they had gone for a brisk walk along the beach, a sea wind whipping against their hair, the water itself too far out to be more than a glimmer of silver-grey spume. Their hunger re-awakened by the tangy air, they had returned to the promenade to eat little saucers of vinegary whelks and orange-yellow cockles. The taste had been delicious and Paula had enjoyed them more than the Whitstable oysters she occasionally sampled. It must be my background coming out in me, she had decided, and wished that success had not made her father grow away from his Northern upbringing.

'My family came from Grimsby,' she had announced suddenly, wiping her fingers on her handkerchief.

'I knew you were real at heart,' Gregory had grinned, and then proceeded to show her what he meant by taking her to the fairground and insisting she sample all it had to offer: from coconut shies to the carousel; from the ghost train to the dodgem cars.

After this they had tea and hot buttered crumpets at another café, before making the return journey to London under a darkening sky peppered with faint stars.

'I'll give you a few hours to rest,' he said, 'and I'll pick you up at eight.'

'You're turning the day into a marathon!'

'We've got tomorrow too!'

She laughed and waved him farewell, wondering where he got his energy from. He looked as fresh now as when he had called for her that morning.

On the gilt and marble table in the hall lay a proof copy of tomorrow's *Sunday Recorder*. It was still damp from the printing press and many sections were left blank, where pictures had not yet been put in. But all the main features were there, including the article on Jack Rossiter. There was a picture of him too. He was older than Paula had assumed—in his early fifties. There was a girl beside him, but she had not come out clearly and it was difficult to guess her age. She took the paper up to her bedroom but did not read it. It had already served its purpose and reminded her that Gregory Scott was putting on as much of an act with her as she was with him. It was an unpalatable thought, but she forced herself to think of it. There was less danger to her peace of mind if she did.

Kicking off her shoes and dumping her clothes on to a chair, she relaxed on the bed. Janet, who had been sitting in her own room at the end of the corridor, came hurrying in.

'A spray of tiger lilies came for you this afternoon,' she said. 'I put them in the refrigerator. But I left the card that came with it on your bedside table.'

Paula reached out for it. As she had expected, it was from Gregory. She frowned. So far she had not called him by his name and waited each time to catch his eye before speaking to him. Yet she thought of him as Gregory and knew how well the word suited his personality. She read the card, then handed it to Janet.

'He wants me to wear a dress to suit the flowers. Can we oblige him?'

Janet went into the dressing-room and returned with a filmy wisp of lemon and apple-green, its tiny bodice held by frail straps. It was one of her Paris dresses, never worn.

Paula regarded it thoughtfully. 'It's very revealing,' she said.

'It's very lovely,' the girl said winningly.

'But it's outdated.'

'Is a beautiful woman ever out of date?' The chiffon fluttered in the breeze of Janet's words. 'A yard of material and a couple of straps. What's there to date in that?'

'Very well, you win.'

'Oh no,' Janet grinned. 'In this dress, *you'll* win!'

CHAPTER SIX

WITH a mixture of emotions Paula waited in the drawing-room for Gregory Scott. The tiger lilies he had sent her graced a small cut-glass vase. She had pinned one to the bodice of her dress but had discarded it as being obvious and put it back with the others.

She wandered over to touch one of the fragile stamens. Even in his choice of flowers, Gregory Scott displayed his sense of humour. Not for her the exotic orchid or the passionate rose. Instead it was the cool pride of the lily and the ferocity of the jungle cat.

Tiger lily. Was that how he thought of her?

'You look exceptionally beautiful,' a crisp voice said, and she spun round to see the man of her thoughts in front of her. He was standing a few feet away, his lids half closed as he surveyed her.

'You startled me,' she explained, afraid he would notice

the quickness of her breathing. 'I didn't hear you come in.'

'I'm sorry. But I wouldn't let your butler announce me. I was curious to see what you look like when you don't know you're being observed.'

His candour was startling. 'Some people would call that prying.'

'I know. But I've made no secret that I want to know everything about you. To that end, I'll use every method I can.'

'Don't you think that total knowledge would lead to total boredom?'

'Not with you. It would lead to contentment and security.'

'That's a great compliment,' she said dryly, and went to the sideboard to pour him a drink. She was glad of the excuse to turn away from him. If eyes could be said to undress, then his had done their work well. Paula had never met a man who made her so aware of her body; and all without saying a word that could not have been over-heard by anyone else. But everything he felt was in the expression in his dark, deep-set eyes, which said so much that made words unnecessary.

With steady movements—at least her father's training counted for something—she poured a whisky and soda and took it over to him. She wore high-heeled shoes and they brought her eyes on a level with his. Fearlessly she stared at him and he returned her gaze. A slight smile quirked one corner of his wide mouth, giving him a faintly sardonic expression and making her wonder if he guessed her thoughts.

'I'm glad you found a dress the colour of the flowers,' he said. 'I wondered if you would take any notice of my request.'

'It was more like a command.'

'No one can command you.'

'My father did.'

'He was a special case.'

'Yes,' she sighed, 'very special.'

'You still miss him, don't you?'

'Very much. Sometimes when I'm at the office I don't feel he's dead.' She hesitated, then said: 'It's almost as if he's still able to communicate with me through the newspapers. Occasionally, when I'm not sure what to do, I sit alone in the office and let my mind drift. I find he always comes to me then, showing me the way.'

'Do you always listen to him?'

'Certainly. Even dead, he's stronger than most men are when they're alive!'

'Are you looking for another strong man to take his place?'

She moved closer to the fireplace. 'I'm not looking for *any* man.'

'Don't you want to get married?'

'If I fall in love,' she shrugged.

'Are you trying not to?'

'What a strange thing to say!'

'I don't see why you think so. You're very much on the defensive with men. You surely know that?'

'I'm only on the defensive with you,' she said quickly, and almost at once saw how he might construe those words. 'I can't forget that Jack Rossiter is your client,' she added.

'Then I'm not making the right impact on you. I'll have to try harder.'

He was close beside her again, almost as close as when they had been dancing. His dinner jacket was undone and she glimpsed the white shirt front. It was a pure silk shirt and through the material she saw the darkness of the hair on his chest. Quickly she lowered her eyes to the maroon cummerbund around his waist. It lent him a swashbuckling air that went well with his erect carriage. He looked as if he held himself on a tight leash, yet at the same time he appeared relaxed. It was an unusual combination and she

was reminded of a cougar lying at ease in the shadows, yet
with all the muscles beneath the glossy coat tensed and
ready to pounce.

'You should throw out all your black dresses,' he said
abruptly.

His words startled her and the glass in her hand jerked,
spilling sherry on her wrist. At once he took the glass away
from her and wiped her hand with a beautifully laundered
handkerchief. Again she noticed how well turned out he
was, and wondered if he had a manservant. She knew little
of his background and even less of his ambitions, yet she
had told him a great deal about herself and had probably
given away even more, without realising it.

Conscious of his nearness, she sat down and then wished
she hadn't, for he remained standing above her, not hiding
the fact that he was scrutinising her. Aware of the lowness
of her bodice, she resisted the urge to lean back in the
chair. But though she remained motionless, she could not
stop a telltale flush from colouring her cheeks.

'You have a beautiful body,' he said matter-of-factly.
'You have no need to hide it.'

'I wasn't aware I did.'

'Even though you wear dreary black dresses with high-
necks and long sleeves? You should choose colour and
fluid fabrics.'

'Are you a dress designer, as well as a lawyer?'

'I know how I like a woman to look.'

The words annoyed her and she tilted her chin. 'I dress
to suit myself.'

'Then you should suit yourself better. You have a
magnificent figure and wonderful skin. Wear colours and
styles to enhance the fact—not detract from it. You're a
tiger lily, Paula. Why dress like a faded fern?'

'Honestly!' she burst out in exasperation.

'Is it *too* honest for you?' he asked whimsically, and
unexpectedly pulled her up from the chair.

Her chiffon skirts swayed around her like wind-tossed leaves, and her quickened breathing made her breasts rise and fall. His eyes rested on the shadowy curve between them before travelling up the smooth shoulders to the graceful neck, the curved chin and the full, wilful mouth. His head bent and she forced herself to remain motionless, wanting him to kiss her but knowing that if he did, she would hit him.

An inch away from her lips, he stopped. 'Get your coat, Paula. We have seats for the theatre.'

Disappointment blotted up her anger; somehow she had not expected such a tame end to this scene.

'What are we going to see?' she asked brightly.

'*Square Circle*.' He named a sophisticated comedy that had recently received rave reviews.

'You took a chance on my not having seen it,' she said as they walked to the front door.

'I also have tickets for the National Theatre. A Restoration comedy had its first night there yesterday.'

Paula could not help being impressed. 'Do you always make contingency plans?'

'Let's say I always like to ensure that my retreats look planned!'

She laughed and settled beside him in his car. What other plans did he have in mind for her, and when was he going to administer the final one? She wondered what he would say when he read tomorrow's article in the *Recorder*, and could not help wishing they had met under different circumstances. Yet without Rossiter he would never have come to her office.

A passing cluster of street lamps silvered the window and threw back her reflection. She looked like a black and white etching, with dramatic angles to her face and a shining sweep of hair. Beautiful almost, she thought with surprise, and wondered whether men would find her so desirable without her material possessions and powers.

With what worldly goods her father had endowed her, yet how poor she was in confidence and all the things that mattered. She swivelled round to the man beside her.

'Have you been married?' she asked abruptly.

'No.'

'Or engaged?'

'Don't tell me you're becoming curious about me?'

'Why shouldn't I be?'

'No reason at all. Except that this is the first time you've asked me any personal questions.' He caught her hand in a warm clasp. 'I was beginning to think you didn't give a damn.'

Paula said nothing and he released her hand and drove in silence for a moment, before speaking.

'To begin with I was too busy concentrating on my career to think of marriage. I told myself I'd wait till I neared the top of the ladder before looking around for someone to share it with me. But by the time I was approaching the final rungs I couldn't find anyone suitable. The older one gets, the more particular one becomes. You see the way your friends' marriages are failing and you start to lose your nerve.'

'I wouldn't have thought you lacked courage,' she commented.

'I'm only a coward when it comes to emotional commitment. Most men are.'

'Yet most men get married.'

'Without committing themselves fully.' His hands gripped the wheel more tightly. 'That isn't the way *I* see marriage. For me it would be all or nothing.'

'All?'

'Total involvement with the woman I love. No secrets, no pretence. Sharing all one's thoughts and emotions.'

'You're asking a great deal,' she said.

'I also have a great deal to give.' He gave her a swift, sidelong look. 'I suppose you think that's conceited of me?'

'It may be very realistic,' she said dryly. 'I don't know you well enough to decide.'

He chuckled. 'Anyway, it's why I'm still single. To me, marriage should be everything. But I never thought it *could be*—until recently.'

Paula tried not to respond to what he was saying. Afraid that he might not be able to get what he wanted from her by appealing to her logic, he was trying to undermine her defences by highly skilful flattery. She longed to tell him she knew what he was doing but forced herself to play dumb. Her victory would be all the sweeter for being delayed.

The theatre came into sight and she was relieved; at least for the next couple of hours she could relax her guard. It would be later—when they were alone—that he would again try to disarm her.

The play was amusing and afterwards they dined at Le Gavroche, where as many of the diners knew Gregory as knew herself. He kept the conversation on an impersonal plane, and soon after midnight he took her home. Expecting him to suggest coming in for a nightcap, she was surprised when he again prepared to leave her at the front door.

'You've had a long day, Paula.'

'You mean I look tired!'

'Tired and particularly beautiful. Fatigue gives you a sensuous lethargy that makes me want to——' He stopped short. 'I'll call for you tomorrow at ten-thirty.'

'Make it an hour later. I like to read all the Sunday papers first.'

He nodded easily, not rising to her remark and then, as he had done on all the other occasions, gave her a casual wave and returned to his car.

Before he could drive away she was inside the house, with the door closed behind her. She had been sure he was going to kiss her goodnight; was positive he had wanted to do so. Yet he had not. Irritably she went to her room. He was playing with her like a skilful fisherman playing a trout: keeping the line relaxed and only prepared to pull it in when he knew the hook had been totally swallowed. What a surprise he would get when she triumphantly spewed it out!

In the morning she found it difficult to concentrate on the newspapers. Her thoughts were with Gregory, trying to guess what his reaction had been when he had seen the *Recorder* and if he had spoken to his client about it. But at eleven-thirty, when he called for her, he seemed as unconcerned as yesterday morning.

'I thought we'd stroll through the park,' he suggested. 'We can listen to the speakers at Hyde Park Corner and then take the day as it comes.'

She swallowed hard. She had not known what she had expected him to say by way of greeting, but it was certainly not this casual comment: as if he had no care in the world.

As always she found him an amusing companion, though most of their walk was taken in silence, striding companionably side by side over the hoary grass. Voices were raised at Speakers Corner, but she listened with only half an ear, too conscious of the man beside her to concentrate on anything or anyone else.

'Had enough?' Gregory asked.

She nodded and he tucked her arm through his and led her away from the crowd.

'Where are we going—Southend?'

'Somewhere nearer and more luxurious,' he smiled. 'My apartment, actually. I've arranged for us to have lunch there.'

She was aware of his bland stare but pretended not to be.

'Fine,' she said gaily. 'I've been wanting to see your pad!'

He laughed. 'Those words don't sit easily on your lips!'

'I know. But at least give me marks for trying.'

'You don't need to try, Paula. Be yourself. You're unique.'

He quickened his pace and she almost had to run to keep up with him, so that she was breathless by the time they reached the quietly elegant block where he lived.

Walking along the carpeted corridor she was conscious only of the heavy beating of her heart. What's the matter with me? she thought. I'm acting like a schoolgirl afraid of being raped. Gregory stopped at a mahogany door, unlocked it and motioned her to proceed him in.

Anticipating something small, luxurious and depersonalised, she was surprised by livable splendour. Antique furniture gleamed with the patina of age and loving care. Comfortable settees and easy chairs, rugs, and well-thumbed books on the shelves that took up almost an entire wall, indicated the many relaxed hours that were spent here.

'What a lovely room,' she exclaimed. 'It doesn't seem like a bachelor's home.'

'What a typically female remark! Just because a man isn't married it doesn't mean he has to live like a pig or a spartan!'

'Rich bachelors usually live in interior decorator splendour,' she retorted, and waved her arm around her. 'But this is neither. It's a real home.'

'As near to a home as one can get in an apartment. I'd prefer a house,' Gregory added, helping her off with her coat. 'But this will do for the moment.'

She curled up in a corner of the settee and appreciatively put out her hands to the log fire which burned in the grate, despite the central heating.

'How extravagant,' she smiled.

'Allow me *one* vice!' He smiled at her. 'I always think a log fire needs a dog and a woman to give it proper life.'

'In that order?'

'The woman comes first!' The glitter in his eyes intensified and he half bent towards her.

'Aren't you going to offer me a drink, Gregory?'

'Sorry.' He straightened and went to the sideboard.

She did not turn her head to watch him, but continued to stare into the fire and hold out her hands to it, hoping she looked the picture of relaxation. His step on the rug was quiet, but she heard it and held up her hand for the glass.

'Martini,' he said. 'I hope it's not too dry.'

She sipped it, and though she tried not to give herself away, he took the glass from her before she could take another sip.

'You're not a gin girl, I see. I should have asked you.'

'I'm not a girl for any short drink,' she said. 'Please don't make me anything else.'

He accepted her refusal without comment and lounged comfortably back in his chair, his legs stretched out to the fireplace. For several moments the only sound was the crackle of logs. The homeliness of the situation unnerved her and she stood up and wandered round the room, only half as interested as she pretended, in looking at the objects and books. These were so diverse that it was difficult to know what his preferences were.

'Where's your cottage in the country?' she asked.

'Near Taplow. But it isn't a cottage, it's a house—a pretty big one with a fair amount of land. At the moment my mother lives there.'

'Your mother!'

'I do have one.' His lips twitched. 'At the risk of spoiling the picture you've obviously built up of me, I must tell you that my brother and I were not orphans, nor did we come from a humble background! It was middle-class and we had a very happy childhood.'

'In Taplow?'

'No. On the Yorkshire moors. We lived there until my father died when I was sixteen. Then we came south.'

He uncrossed his legs and she saw the muscles flex along his thighs. Quickly she averted her gaze. 'So the house in Taplow is not the ancestral home?'

'It may be for future Scotts,' he grinned. 'I bought it eight years ago, after my first big and successful case. My mother's only waiting for me to get married so that she can move into a little cottage on the estate; near enough to keep an eye on the children when my wife and I are too busy to get down.'

Paula found it all too easy to see the picture he was painting. 'You have everything planned, haven't you?'

'I told you I don't like being caught unawares.'

She avoided his probing glance, and trying to be casual about it, inadvertently brushed against the table. A pile of newspapers lay on it, the top one the *Sunday Recorder*. She glanced at the front page, then looked at Gregory. He was watching her, his body still relaxed in the chair, his wide shoulders almost masking the back. He looked more like a pugilist than a city lawyer, and she knew that in this lay his strength.

'I assume you've read today's article?' she asked. Her voice was not as cool as she would have liked and her hands were tingling. Afraid they might start to shake, she dug them into the pockets of her skirt.

'I got a copy at two o'clock this morning,' he replied.

'If I'd known you were so anxious to read it I could have let you have my proof copy. It was sent to me on Saturday afternoon. I suppose you're furious at what we wrote?'

'My client is.' With a lithe movement he rose. It brought him close to her and again she could feel the warmth radiating from him.

'I hate what your newspaper is doing to Jack,' he said roughly, 'and it's going to cost you your shirt.'

'Me?' she queried.

'Grayson Publications.'

'Oh.' Paula moistened her lips. 'For a moment you made it sound so personal that I wasn't sure what——'

'I'm doing my damnedest to divide you into two,' he interrupted her roughly, 'but it isn't easy.'

She edged away from him. 'You still maintain that Rossiter's innocent?'

'Yes.'

She waited for him to continue, searching his face for some sign of anger. But there was only a strange look of resignation on it.

'You still think I'm taking you out because of Jack, don't you?' he said. 'That because I couldn't use my ability as a lawyer to get you to print a retraction, I decided to seduce you with my charm and manliness?'

'It had entered my head,' she admitted lightly.

'Don't pretend with me, Paula.' His voice was blunt. 'You've thought of nothing else since you started to see me. Well, I'm sorry to disappoint you, but my asking you to come out with me had nothing to do with Jack. When I saw you the first time at the opera, I knew I had to see you again. Walking into your office the next day and finding you there was the greatest stroke of luck.'

'It certainly was,' she commented. 'Otherwise you might never have found me again. Or were you going to haunt the Opera House?'

'JBDL 43,' he said.

'JB what?'

'The number plate of your car. I made sure I was directly behind you when you left the theatre.'

'I didn't notice you,' she said coldly, sure she would have done so had three people been following her.

'That wasn't the intention,' he said whimsically. 'My chauffeur drove my guests to the Savoy and I followed your car and took the number.'

'It was Guy's car.'

'I knew I could find you through him. You didn't give the impression that it was your first date with him!'

Shaken by what she had learned, Paula sat down. Her hair fell forward and hid her face and his hand came out to push the heavy waves back.

'You're so unaware of the power you have over me,' he said huskily. 'And I was determined not to let you know it until I could convince you it had nothing to do with who you are.' With a sharp movement he pulled her up and into his arms. 'I wish to God I didn't know Jack Rossiter! I wish we could have met like two ordinary people. *Paula*.'

Her name was almost a cry, stifled as his mouth came fiercely down on hers. For an instant she stiffened in his hold, resenting the pressure of his touch, then relaxed against him, surrendering to him in a way she had never done to any man. Feeling her pliancy, his lips softened, moving gently over hers until they parted for him. The pressure increased again, but it was a pleasurable one and roused her into an awareness of her body. He felt the tremor that went through her, and his hands slid slowly down her back to her waist and then up again to cup her breasts. Involuntarily she resisted the touch and he pushed her a little away from him and smiled into her eyes.

'My tiger lily's a blushing violet,' he teased.

'Are you surprised!'

'I'm pleased.'

He did not say why and she did not ask him. There was no need. He was a man who would always want to be the first; whether it was in his professional life or his personal one.

With a sigh she rested her head upon his shoulder. One of his hands came up to stroke her hair and she felt the muscles move in his shoulders. She lowered her head further still and heard the heavy thudding of his heart. The sound of it made him seem vulnerable and she felt a surge of tenderness towards him. Putting up her hands, she touched the side of his face, then let her fingers move up his temple to the crisp dark hair.

'Paula?' He tilted her chin until their eyes met.

'Yes, Gregory.'

His arm tightened around her and his body seemed to become her bulwark. 'Do you know that's only the second time you've ever said my name? Say it again.'

'Gregory.' She repeated it a third time. 'It suits you. It's strong and—and different.'

'I'm certainly different with *you*,' he replied humorously. 'With any other woman I'd have been in the bedroom by now!'

A stab of jealousy went through her, followed by anger at the insensitivity of his remark. Did he have to spoil this moment by mentioning the other women he had had?

'My tiger lily's become a catkin,' he said with amusement. 'You look as if you're getting ready to hiss! Didn't you like my mentioning the other women in my life?'

'It hardly seems the appropriate time.'

'I wasn't going to pretend that you'd be the first!'

'I——'

'And forget them. They meant nothing. All they've done is to make me appreciate *you*.'

'You can't say that until.... I mean you—you haven't——'

'I don't need to have you with my body in order to have you with my mind,' he said huskily. 'And my mind's been working overtime since the minute I met you!'

Once more he sought her mouth. It was hard to believe that lips that could look so hard could kiss with such softness. With a subtlety that amazed her, he showed his expertise as a lover, knowing when to demand and when to give in. Without being aware of it, she found herself on the settee with him, her body below his, his weight forcing her back against the cushions. But his mouth was still soft, cajoling her with infinite patience into a less inhibited response.

Desire swamped her fear and she abandoned herself to his touch, widening her arms to clasp him closer; her limbs relaxing the better to feel him. Deeper and deeper he seemed to penetrate her, until her entire body was aflame with the need for him. He thrust forward upon her, his chest a banner of steel, his thighs throbbing with urgency. On the brink of total surrender she gave a cry and tried to push him away, and at the very same instant he drew back. Poised above her, Gregory gazed deep into her eyes, then carefully eased himself away from her.

'Perfect unison of timing,' he said thickly. 'It augurs well for the future.'

Her blush was vivid and with a muttered exclamation he gathered her close and hugged her.

'Darling Paula! I can see I'll have you changing colour more often than a chameleon!'

'Not once I'm used to you,' she said, and coloured even more vividly as she realised what she had said.

But it was impossible to be embarrassed with him when it felt so right to be in his arms, and she snuggled close and closed her eyes, content to remain where she was.

Time passed. The logs flared and splintered, showering the hearthstone with scarlet sparks that swiftly turned to grey. Gregory stirred and sighed with contentment and she tilted her head and looked at him.

'Why didn't you kiss me until today?'

'Because I was determined to wait until you'd published your final article about Jack. Then you wouldn't be able to say I'd tried to seduce you into changing your editorial policy.'

His words pleased her, though she had to answer him truthfully. 'It mightn't be our last article on him. Once you start uncovering something you don't always know where or when it will end.' She felt the tenseness in him, but when he spoke his voice was still relaxed.

'The *Recorder* will go on doing its job and so will I.'

'Does that mean you're going to sue me?' She pulled slightly away from him.

'I'll sue Grayson Publications,' he said harshly. 'Never you!' Violently he pulled her down again, then swung over so that he was lying on top of her. 'Kiss me,' he demanded. 'Kiss me and stop talking!'

Afterwards, Paula looked on that as one of the happiest days of her life. Certainly the day on which she awakened as a woman and saw all the possibilities it held for her.

They lunched together in the small dining-room off the main sitting-room, though she was not conscious of anything she ate. Then they returned to the fireside and talked and made love again. It was obvious Gregory wanted her completely, yet he made no attempt to seduce her nor even to persuade her. She marvelled at his control but recognised it as a part of his character and thought longingly of the time when neither of them need be on guard any longer.

'I suppose you must think I'm very old-fashioned,' she said, when he gave a muttered exclamation and pulled his mouth away from hers.

'Yes,' he said tersely, 'I do.'

There was silence.

'Are you surprised?' she ventured.

'Why should I be? I knew when I met you that you were a surprising woman!'

'You're a surprising man.'

'Because I've got patience with you?' He gave her a slight shake. 'You cast me as Mephistopheles and you don't like to admit you're wrong!'

'Never Mephistopheles,' she protested. 'Casanova perhaps, but——'

'Not Casanova either. I'm too busy to waste my time chasing women.'

'Do *they* chase you?'

'Generally.'

'Oh.'

'Don't say "oh" in that way. Don't you like to know that other females find me exciting?'

She was not sure if he was serious or teasing, and as if he guessed it he gave her another shake, less gentle than the first.

'I don't need to rush you, Paula. If you were willing, you would find me ready and very able! But as you're not....'

'It's the way I was brought up,' she said on a sigh. 'My father had very strong ideas on the subject.'

'Your father had strong ideas on many subjects.'

'You sound as if you knew him.'

'When I look at you, I feel as if I did.'

'I'm not sure I like that remark,' she said. 'It makes me seem like his shadow.'

'In some ways I think you are. You run your papers the way *he'd* want you to run them, and if you've any doubts about what to do, you wait for him to give you guidance. You said so yourself.'

'I didn't mean it quite so literally.'

'I think you did.' He moved his body and lay partially across her again. 'But don't apologise for it, Paula. Even a man in your position would have found him intimidating.'

'If that were so, I'd have been quick to change the minute he died.'

'Intimidating *and* indoctrinating,' Gregory said.

'No!'

'Then come to bed with me.'

The demand took her by surprise, but before she could formulate an answer, Gregory spoke.

'See what I mean? If you were truly your own woman, you'd have been mine an hour ago! But as you're not....'

'Very clever,' she scoffed.

'Very patient,' he replied, and stilled her reply with his mouth.

Patient as well as clever, she thought, and wished he were a little less of both.

CHAPTER SEVEN

RON SMITH and Guy were waiting for Paula when she entered her office on Monday morning.

Guilty at having turned down Guy's invitation on Saturday, she gave him an extra warm smile. He did not respond to it and she wondered if he knew that she had seen Gregory Scott. He had the knack of finding out what she was doing and, if he felt threatened by it, would go out of his way to assert his relationship with her; as he was now doing by incisively placing a typewritten letter in front of her.

'From your friend Mr Scott,' he said coldly.

Paula read it through quickly. In brusque terms it stated that the *Recorder*'s articles on Jack Rossiter were defamatory and that legal action would be taken unless a public retraction and financial compensation were made. It was dated that morning and had been sent round by hand. There was nothing conciliatory in the tone of the letter and she was fiercely glad that Gregory had not allowed his personal feelings for her to colour his business ones. She would try to act in the same way; the Gregory Scott whom Grayson Publications would fight was not the man she loved.

The man she loved. How easily the acknowledgement came into her mind, and how right it felt. She had never believed love would come upon her so quickly, nor that it would be for a man as vital as Gregory. Theirs would not be an easy relationship. They were both strong-willed and neither of them would accept anything less than total honesty and involvement. But then that was why they were still unmarried; why she had never been able to marry Guy.

With an effort she brought her mind back to the letter. 'What's our next move?' she asked.

'We write back and say we won't retract a single word.'

'And then?'

'Then we brief the best barrister we can get. A barrister and a silk,' Guy added. 'Scott will make a fight of this, and we must be ready to hit hard.'

'You really believe Rossiter will want the publicity of a court case?'

Guy's eyes were hard as sun-bright pebbles. 'Anyone who wanted to compromise or be conciliatory would never use Scott as their lawyer. He's made his name on hard, tough litigation.'

'I don't believe he'd fight without a cause,' Paula said.

'He's the type of lawyer who makes the cause.'

'We've nothing to worry about,' Ron Smith said. 'Jack Rossiter's guilty and we can prove it.'

'Weaver Brothers won't be happy about a court action.' Guy ignored the interruption. 'It will mean bringing up a lot of things they'd prefer to keep hidden.'

'Such as?' Paula asked.

'Their own espionage set-up.'

'The whole business stinks,' she said flatly. 'I wish we hadn't started it.' An image of her father came so strongly into her mind that she sat up straight. 'No, I don't mean that,' she amended. 'It's been an excellent series and it's done wonders for our circulation. It's just that I loathe litigation.' She looked at Ron. 'Does Rossiter's name appear in the next article?'

'Why?' he demanded. 'Are you getting cold feet?'

She flushed, but Guy spoke to her before she could answer.

'If we aren't going to print an apology and pay damages, we might as well go on to the end.'

'As long at it's the truth.'

'Do you want me to sign that in blood?' Ron Smith asked angrily.

'I'll have every pint, if you're proved wrong!' Paula looked down at Gregory's letter, then up at Guy. 'How do you suggest we deal with this?'

'I'll write and tell Scott to do his damnedest—in legal terminology, of course.'

'That won't frighten him off.'

'It may make him think again. He knows damn well his client hasn't got a case. If Rossiter's faced with paying *our* costs too, Scott will whistle for his fee.'

'I believe Rossiter's a personal friend of his,' Paula said evenly, 'so he might not be doing it for the money.'

Guy glanced at Ron Smith, and the editor, taking the hint, left them.

'You've been seeing quite a lot of Gregory Scott, haven't you?' Guy said as soon as they were alone.

'Do you have someone spying on me?' she asked lightly.

'I love you,' he replied, 'and I make it my business to know the opposition.'

'I don't find that very flattering.' She spun round in her chair and faced the window. 'I don't like being watched and I'd appreciate it if you'd stop.'

'Don't be silly, Paula. You know I don't spy on you. A friend of mine happened to see you with Scott at the Starlight Room and I saw you myself with him on Sunday in the park.'

'You should have come over and said hello.'

'From the way you were looking at each other I felt I'd be in the way.' Guy came round the side of the desk to stand beside her. 'I don't know what game he's playing with you, but——'

'What makes you think he's playing a game?' she asked.

'Why else is he seeing you?'

'Thanks!'

'Dash it, Paula, you know what I mean. The man's notorious for his love affairs and——'

'Maybe he wants one with me. Or don't you think that's possible?'

Guy reddened. 'I'm not minimising your attraction. I —er—I'm merely trying to make you see that Scott doesn't usually go for intelligent, high-powered women. He prefers them dumb and beautiful.'

'So do most men.'

'But Scott even more than most!'

Paula swung back to face the desk. 'You seem to know a lot about him.'

Guy shrugged. 'You know what it's like at the club. Men talk.'

'More than women, it seems!'

'Lord Belling's ex-wife—she was an actress—was his mistress for two years, and Andrea Hardy, the singer, was before that.'

'I'm not interested in Gregory's affairs,' Paula said icily. 'I'm busy, Guy. Go play the serpent in another garden.'

'Don't tell me you're in Paradise with Scott!'

'You're doing your best to make sure I'm not.'

'I'm doing my best to stop you making a fool of yourself. What's the matter with you? You've only known the man a week!'

He reached out and grabbed her. Because he was rarely demonstrative, she was taken by surprise and did not resist him.

'For God's sake, Paula, can't you see the game he's playing? He finds you attractive—most men would—but he's also out to use you.'

She toyed with the idea of telling him about the number plate of the car, then decided against it. In his present frame of mind, Guy was not prepared to hear anything about Gregory—unless it was bad. He was still holding her and she became aware of the way his hands were trembling. It lessened her anger and she moved gently away from his grasp.

'Please, Guy, I don't want to talk about it any more.'

'Are you in love with him?' he demanded.

'I don't want to discuss it.'

'You at least owe me an answer.'

'I don't know the answer,' she lied.

'Very well.' He picked up Gregory's letter. 'You're obviously infatuated with the man and I'll give you time to get over it. You're too sensible not to see him for what he is—eventually.'

Long after Guy had gone, his words lingered in the room like evil spirits, disquieting her for the rest of the day and only disappearing when Gregory called for her later that evening to take her out.

She did not see him again for the rest of the week, for they were both busy; he with a case which necessitated his flying to the Bahamas, and she with several business meetings which went on till late each night. Someone was buying shares in the company and had already acquired a sizeable holding; not enough to give them control, but enough to make them dangerous should they link forces with any other of the big shareholders.

During the endless discussions that took place upon the subject, when they sought for ways and means of thwarting such a happening, Paula was grateful for Guy's help. She knew he did not agree with her desire to retain control of the company, and that he wanted her to accept the next good bid that came their way. But as long as she *did* retain control she knew she could rely on his support. However, it did not prevent him from airing his opinion when they were alone.

'If you were keen on empire-building,' he said as he

drove her home on Thursday evening, 'I'd say you were wise to go it alone. But you're not ambitious—in the tycoon sense of the word.'

'I've brought out new magazines.'

His shrug made the project unimportant.

'What would I do if I retired?' she asked.

'Enjoy yourself. With me, I hope. But if not, then with —with someone worthy of you.'

'I'm already enjoying myself—as well as running a business. I don't need to give up one in order to do the other.'

'At least take things more easily,' he persisted. 'Sell out but still remain in the company.'

'A queen without a throne doesn't happen to be my idea of power,' she said drily.

'I thought you weren't interested in power?'

'I'm not.'

'Then why are you so determined to retain it?'

'Because my father built Graysons from nothing, and I've no intention of letting it go.'

'It would still continue.'

'It wouldn't be *his* company any more.'

'It isn't his company now. It's yours.'

She sighed. 'I don't feel it's mine.'

'I know. That's one more reason why you should sell out.'

They were back where they had started, and she could not deny the truth of what he had said. Instead, she challenged the business sense of it.

'If we're good enough for someone to want to buy us, then surely we're good enough to expand on our own?'

'Of course we are. But we'd need double the capital we've got. And the only way to get it is to borrow.'

'I hate borrowing. My father always——' She stopped, but not before Guy had seen his opening.

'Then bring in a partner—someone with money. With a

stronger Board and double the capital, Grayson's could be the biggest group in the country.'

'I'll think about it,' she promised and, true to her word, did so as she lay soaking in a warm bath.

But she was too tired to give it serious consideration and she thankfully climbed into bed and relaxed against the pillows. What would her life be like without the newspapers? Her thoughts meandered on, only returning to the present as her private telephone rang. Like an excited schoolgirl she answered it, hoping it would be Gregory. It was and, as always, she thrilled to the sound of his voice.

'How's my tycoon?' he teased.

'Tired. It's been a long day.'

'For me too. I'll be glad when I'm home.'

'When are you coming back?' she asked.

'Tomorrow.'

'Was your trip successful?'

'Of course.'

'Of course,' she mimicked. 'Don't you ever have a failure?'

'We're still talking about my work, I assume?'

She hesitated.

'I bet you've gone pink,' he said. 'I wish I was there to see it.'

'It's mean of you to tease me.'

'I'd like to be much meaner,' he said roughly. 'You bring out the brute in me.'

She laughed softly. 'Be serious, Gregory.'

'What makes you think I'm not?' He echoed her laugh. 'How do you feel about a weekend in a lovely cottage in Suffolk?'

It had come. Anticipated, half wanted and half feared, and she still did not know what to say.

'Well, madame, is it yes or no?'

'Just you and me?'

'And the Parishes. They live in the cottage and they're great friends of mine.'

'I see.'

'*Now* you do.' His answer told her he knew the reason for her hesitation. 'Tom's a naturalist and runs a bird sanctuary, and Jean writes children's books. They'd love to meet you. We can leave late on Friday afternoon and get there in time for dinner. It will be my last chance of seeing them until the autumn. They're going to India next week.'

'I'd like to come with you,' she said quickly. 'It will be a pleasure to get out of London.'

'I'll collect you at five,' he said. 'But I may be late. I'm seeing Guy Ardrey as soon as I get in from the airport, and the meeting might go on for a while. He's a tough opponent.'

'He says the same of you.'

There was a snort at the end of the line and Paula laughed and quickly said goodnight, afraid that if the conversation turned to Jack Rossiter, it would sour the mood. One day she and Gregory would have to talk the whole thing out. But not until the case was settled. On this thought she fell asleep.

Late Friday afternoon found her waiting at home for Gregory's arrival. She had left the office soon after lunch and only her secretary knew where she could be contacted if an emergency arose. 'Your newspaper is your child,' her father had warned her, 'and you must never forget you owe it first call on your time.' But now she knew that Gregory came first, and that she would happily give up a full-time career in order to be his wife and have his children. Guy's wish for her to sell out might come sooner than he expected.

Nervously she paced the drawing-room. It was madness to think in such concrete terms when Gregory had still made no mention of their future. Yet why should he? They had only known each other a short time—far too short for him to commit himself. On his own admission he enjoyed being a bachelor and might still have no wish to settle down.

Unexpectedly she remembered the names of the two women Guy had flung at her. According to him, one of them had been his mistress for two years. The thought that Gregory had cared sufficiently for a woman to stay with her for that length of time, yet not marry her, was a frightening indication of his desire to remain free. If he still felt the same, how would their own relationship proceed? She could not see herself being happy in the role of girl-friend.

His step in the hall precluded further thought and she was standing calmly by the mantelpiece when he came in. Across the room their eyes met and her heart began to beat as fast as if she had been running.

'Each time I see you, you look more beautiful.' His voice was crisp, as if he were trying to remain aloof from his words.

'You make it sound more of an indictment than a compliment!'

'It *is* an indictment. I resent your hold over me.'

She flung out her hands. 'I'm not holding you, Gregory.'

'You are,' he said, and touched his hand to his chest. 'Here.'

She felt a thrill of triumph but knew better than to show it. 'Would you like to change your weekend plans? I'd be quite happy not to see you.'

'Would you indeed?' In two strides he was beside her, and she was being kissed with a fervency that left her breathless.

'*Now* would you be quite happy to change your weekend plans?' he demanded.

'I was thinking of *your* happiness,' she countered.

'That depends on you, my dear Paula.' Catching her hand, he walked with her to the door.

Her suitcase stood in the hall; a small leather one, with her initials on the side, in gold. Gregory eyed it and then picked it up.

'I'm glad you aren't the type to take masses of luggage,' he said.

'Only because I'm a demon for buying things when I get to my destination! My father was like that too. We once went to Rome for a weekend and only took some toothpaste. We bought everything else when we got there!'

Gregory was still laughing at this as they got into the car. It was the same one he had used to take her to Southend last Saturday. Incredible to think it was only a week ago. She felt as if she had known him a lifetime. Panic rose in her. It was dangerous to let herself get so involved with him. She should never have accepted this invitation. But it still wasn't too late to change her mind. She could plead a migraine; or work to do. She could even tell him the truth and say she would rather stay for the evening only.

The car pulled away from the kerb and she gave a deep sigh and settled back in the seat.

'Crisis over?' he asked.

'What crisis?'

'The one that had you clenching your hands and perching on the edge of the seat.'

'Don't be silly. I was just wondering if I'd left anything behind.'

Gregory gave a shout of laughter. 'After what you said about that trip to Rome? You'll have to lie better than that!'

Reluctantly she smiled. 'The Roman shops are probably better equipped than the village where we're going.'

'Too true.' His tone showed her he was still amused, but he was too clever to continue with the subject and switched on the cassette recorder. The strains of Jerome Kern's 'A Fine Romance' filtered into the air.

'Mood music,' she said solemnly. 'How clever of you.'

'I knew you'd appreciate it.'

Their eyes met, both pairs amused, yet with something deeper flickering in them. Paula felt suspended; as if she were poised on a roller-coaster waiting for the downward swoop. She lowered her lids and stared at her hands, white and ringless on her lap. Would Gregory put a ring there? If he didn't, it wouldn't be for want of her trying. It was her first admission that she wanted him enough to fight for him. The knowledge was comforting. She was a good fighter, her father had made her that, and she would do him proud all over again.

CHAPTER EIGHT

RAIN began to fall as they left London, increasing to a steady downpour as they drove through the suburbs and becoming a torrent once they reached open country.

'Sorry about this,' Gregory apologised as he almost drew to a stop to peer through the windscreen. 'If I'd known the weather was going to deteriorate I would have called for you earlier.'

'I don't mind,' Paula said honestly, snug and warm beneath the rug he had draped over her.

'You don't, do you?' His look warmed her even further. 'I'm always surprised how good-tempered you are. You look such a firebrand.'

'A tiger lily,' she corrected.

'More lily than tiger at the moment,' he chuckled, and put his foot on the accelerator again.

They drove for a while in silence before she asked him what time his friends were expecting them.

'No fixed time,' he replied. 'If they have to go out they leave the key in a hiding place near the porch.'

'Do you go there often?'

'Once a month or so.'

'You've never spoken of them before.'

'I've been too busy talking about you.'

She smiled. 'I wish you'd talk more about *yourself*. You're still a stranger to me.'

He drew her hand to his lips and held it there for a moment. 'I haven't kissed you like a stranger.' He rubbed his tongue along the edge of her fingers.

Paula shivered at the contact and quickly pulled her hand away. 'There's more to intimacy than kissing.'

'There certainly is,' he said so fervently that she laughed. 'Does your mind always turn to sex?'

'No more than most males,' he retorted. 'But I've been particularly restrained with *you*.'

'Particularly bearing in mind your reputation,' she said.

'Tell me about my reputation.'

His remark took her unawares and she was quiet. He said no more and she knew he was waiting for her to answer him.

'Some of your love affairs have made the gossip columns,' she said, fervently hoping this to be true. 'Jean Belling and—and Andrea Hardy, to name but two.'

'Does my past worry you?' he asked.

'It interests me.'

'You may ask me any questions you like.'

'I thought gentlemen didn't kiss and tell?'

'I've no intention of telling.'

'Then why encourage me to ask?' she said indignantly.

'Because I'm curious to find out what's in your mind!'

'Now you've condemned me to eternal silence on the subject!'

'Thank God for that!'

She giggled. 'You're incorrigible!'

'That's what my nanny used to say to me when I was six.'

'And it still applies—which at least shows you're consistent.'

'Consistent and faithful.'

'For how long?'

The question hovered between them for so long that she had decided Gregory was not going to answer it, when he did.

'For as long as I remain interested. I enjoy sex and I've made no secret of it. But I've always avoided one-night stands. There's something cheapening about them.'

'I can understand that.'

'Sometimes my affairs have lasted a year, sometimes less. With Jean it was longer.'

'Did you never——'

'No,' he interrupted. 'I never wanted to marry her. We began as friends and we ended as friends.'

'What happened to her?' she asked.

'Jean's living in the States and Andrea's married and expecting a child.'

Another question rose to her lips, but she refused to give it utterance.

'It's two years since I saw either of them,' he continued evenly. 'Since then I've been fairly celibate.'

'That isn't a word you can qualify.'

He chuckled. 'Are you ever at a loss for something to say?'

'Not if I can help it.'

She buried her chin in her collar and waited for him to speak again. Instead he concentrated on the road, which was narrow and undulating. Disappointed that he was not going to say more, Paula wished she could read his mind as easily as he seemed able to read hers. Guy was right when he said Gregory was a tough, hard man. But he was a subtle one too, and that made him extremely dangerous.

The car slowed and they moved forward almost at walking pace. She realised why when she felt it judder, and knew that the surface of the road was not tarmacked. There was a particularly vicious jolt and her head bumped against the roof.

'Sorry,' Gregory apologised. 'Rain plays havoc with this lane.'

'Where's the cottage?'

'At the end of it.'

She peered through the windscreen but could not see anything.

'You'll see it in a minute,' he said. 'It's round the next bend.'

They turned it and, through the mist and gloom, Paula made out a steep roof and two slender chimneys. Everything was in darkness and even when they had stopped the car and hurried up the path to the door, no one came out to greet them.

'Your friends can't be here,' she said, and tried to see the time on her watch. The little diamond numbers glinted and she guessed it to be nearly eight o'clock.

'They might have gone to the pub,' Gregory said cheerily, and rooting under the porch, straightened with a large key in his hand.

'We can let ourselves in.' He proceeded to do so and Paula stepped into the blackness.

There was a click and lamps glowed into life. Paula saw they were in a small hall, facing an archway that led to a sitting-room which appeared to take up the whole width and breadth of the cottage. The kitchen was part of the room too, being an open-plan one and beautifully fitted with pine cupboards and steel worktops. Tom Parish must be a financially independent naturalist, she decided, taking in the rustic charm of the furniture and the expensive-looking sofas that stood either side of a vast chimney breast. She stepped closer and looked at the fire grate. It was laid for a fire but was unlit. She glanced at Gregory and saw him looking at the fireplace too, his expression tense.

'Are you sure your friends know we're coming?' she asked.

'Certainly. Tom called me ten days ago and I said I'd come down this weekend.' His brows drew together, making her suddenly aware of his nose, beaky and strong. 'I didn't actually confirm it with him. I dropped him a note.'

'Perhaps he didn't get it.'

He stepped back into the hall and she saw him stop by a small oak table. 'He didn't,' he said in a strange voice, and came towards her holding an unopened envelope, as well as several others. 'Their mail for the past week—if the dates are anything to go by.'

Paula swallowed nervously. 'Do you mean they aren't here?'

'It looks like it.'

He frowned again and, putting the letters down, rummaged in his breast pocket for a small leather diary. He leafed through it and the frown turned to a scowl.

'Damn!' he raised his head. 'You'll want to murder me, darling, but I've slipped up by a week. They left for India *last* Friday, not next Friday, as I thought.'

'Oh, Gregory!' Paula looked at him helplessly and then began to laugh.

The sound smoothed away the tension on his face. His own laughter echoed in the room and he put his arms round her shoulders and hugged her.

'You're an angel not to be furious with me.' He felt her shiver and immediately drew back and knelt to put a match to the fire in the grate.

'It's a pity to light it,' she said.

'There's no point in our freezing to death. We might as well warm ourselves for a bit. We've a long drive back.'

Paula glanced through the leaded panes. It was still raining heavily and a gale seemed to have blown up too, for it moaned and whistled against the cottage walls.

'I suggest we have something to eat before we leave,'

said Gregory. 'Jean usually keeps the larder well stocked with tins.'

Paula watched as he walked over to the kitchen and began opening cupboards. There was a wonderful array of food in them, from soup, paté and duck in orange sauce to tinned fruit and vacuum-packed coffee.

'Get yourself warm while I fix us a meal,' he said, and gave her a little push in the direction of the fire, which was now burning brightly.

'Let me help you,' she protested.

'Don't tell me you can cook?'

'I can open a tin as well as you!' It was her turn to give him a push. 'You've done the driving, Gregory. Let *me* prepare a meal.'

He nodded without any protest and she saw he was unusually pale. There were lines around his eyes, as though he had not slept well, and his eyelids were dark, which increased the pallor of his face.

'Have a rest,' she repeated, and waited for him to walk past her to the sofa nearest the fire.

Quickly and quietly she set to work, grateful for the Paris cookery course which her father had made her take when she had written a cookery column for six months. Searching among the drawers she found cutlery and place settings. She laid the table, checked to see everything was ready and then walked over to Gregory. He was fast asleep.

It was the first time she had seen him so defenceless and she stared at him intently. Lines of tension were still visible on his forehead but his mouth was relaxed, which made the lower lip appear fuller. His cheeks were slightly flushed from his proximity to the fire and his head had fallen back against the arm of the settee. His hair was ruffled and a lock had fallen across his temples, making him look younger and rather vulnerable. Yet even so, he looked a man to be reckoned with. Paula bent towards him, and as she did so his eyes opened, bright as a bird's. She stared into their brown depths and felt as if she were drowning in them.

'S-supper's ready,' she stammered.

'Fine. I'll just go and wash.'

'I'd like to do the same.'

He caught her hand and led her up the narrow flight of stairs.

This part of the cottage was larger than she had expected and she saw that extra space had been built over the garage. There were three bedrooms; two with their own bathrooms and one with a wash-basin. The larger one she took to belong to the Parishes and Gregory motioned her to take the other one. The room was cold, but there was towel and soap in the bathroom and she tidied herself and was downstairs in the kitchen when Gregory joined her. He had changed into a sweater and it made him look boyish and carefree.

It was a mood that lasted through their meal and he complimented her outrageously on her ability as a cook.

'You open the best tinned duck of any woman I've met.'

'I wish I could say the same about your wine,' she teased, and heard him give an exclamation of disgust as he rose and disappeared from the room.

He returned after a moment with a dusty bottle.

'It should be claret with duck,' he apologised. 'But it was far too cold to use. So we'll have a Chablis instead.'

Later, as they sipped the rest of their wine in front of the blazing logs, Paula said she felt like Goldilocks.

Gregory gave her a sardonic glance. 'We won't play out the whole story, though. There'll be no question of who's been sleeping in my bed!'

Embarrassed, she moved away from his encircling arm and made a pretence of raking the fire. 'I suppose we should be thinking of getting back.'

'Yes,' he said, and yawned prodigiously as he stood up. Even in the muted glow from the single standard lamp they had left alight, he looked desperately tired. Heavy lines had carved themselves on either side of his mouth and his expression was strained.

'Don't you feel well?' she asked anxiously.

'I'm tired,' he confessed. 'It's been a hard week and I think I'm suffering from jet lag.'

'Then it was silly of you to drive all the way down here.' She was annoyed at her own stupidity for not having prevented him. 'You should cut down before you drop down.'

'I keep telling myself that.' He drew her up beside him. 'Let's forget the outside world for sixty seconds. Right now it's just you and me. Two people in isolation, with nothing to think about except each other.'

It was a wonderful thought and though she knew it could not last, she wanted to savour it while it did. She snuggled against him. His shoulders were broad and gave her the feeling that she had found a safe harbour. She had kicked off her shoes a little earlier and her eyes were on a level with his mouth. It was quirked in a smile and she put her fingers to it and traced the line of his upper lip.

'Let's stay a bit longer,' she whispered, and pulled him back on to the sofa. For an instant she had the impression Gregory was going to resist, then with a murmur his arms tightened around her.

The flames glowed, but it was nothing to the flame that sprang up between them. It burned them with its intensity, threatening to dissolve all barriers of convention. In a frenzy of desire Paula opened her mouth to his. The strain of the past week, when she had pored over figures until she was blinded by them, had taken its toll of her. She wanted to be enveloped by his strength; longed for the relief of total abandon, of knowing she had no more decisions to make, no more problems to solve. She would leave them to Gregory, to this strong, powerful man to whom she wanted to devote her life.

'Dearest,' she whispered, and caught his head between her hands.

His eyes burned into hers, coming closer and closer until they blotted out everything. His body lay directly on her and she felt the weight of it. Her limbs were shaking, dissolving with the intensity of her desire as his hands wound themselves around her hair, pulling it back from her face so that his lips could bury themselves in the softness of the skin behind her ear. Slowly his mouth travelled along the nape of her neck to rest upon the fragile collar bone. His hands moved down her shoulders and he unzipped her dress and gently cupped her breasts. She shivered and pulled him closer still, feeling his body swell as she did so. She knew she was playing with fire, but she did not care.

'Gregory,' she moaned, and rubbed against him, her nipples stiff with desire.

He gave a convulsive movement and then began to pull off his sweater and tear open his shirt. His chest was bare save for the thick hair that lay along the centre and she arched upwards until her body touched it.

'Paula,' he groaned. 'Do you know what you're doing?'

'Love me,' she begged, and spread her fingers along his spine.

His cry was sharp and he fell upon her in a frenzy, forcing her head back into the cushions. Hungrily she clung to him, oblivious of everything except her need of him; her urge to be possessed. The deep emotions of her ancestors rose up to envelop her. She was no longer Paula Grayson of the seventies but primitive woman—linked by her genes to the cave-woman of the past.

'No!' The cry was wrenched from him, and like a man in a daze he pulled away from her and went to stand by the fire.

Still drugged by passion, she lay and watched him. 'What's wrong, Gregory?'

'Nothing. That's the trouble. It's all too right.'

He turned and bent over her. The fire had burned itself out, but it was still bright enough for her to see his face. It was flushed and his eyes were narrowed as though he was in pain.

'You're not well,' she said, and sat up quickly, putting out her hands to him.

Instantly he straightened. 'It's late, Paula. We should be leaving.'

She glanced at the dishes stacked in the sink. 'I have to wash up first.'

'No!' He almost shouted the word. 'We must go.'

'But——'

'Come on,' he repeated. 'Let's go while I've still got the strength to take you.'

Involuntarily she smiled. 'I don't think you do have the strength to take me! You're too tired.'

Almost against his will he smiled too. 'You're a witch,' he whispered. 'You know damn well what I meant.'

'Yes,' she admitted. 'And you surprise me. I thought I'd have to fight for my honour, instead of which I feel as if I'm fighting to lose it!'

'Come on,' he said, half tenderly, half roughly, and strode to the door.

She was beside him as he opened it and staggered back as the gale force wind almost tore the door from his hand. He slammed it shut again and swore under his breath.

'We'd better be quick or the lane will be impassable. I once got bogged down there in the car and had to be pulled out with a tractor.'

Remembering their bumpy ride down the lane Paula did not doubt this, and the thought that had been in her mind from the moment she had known the Parishes were not here reasserted itself.

'Why can't we sleep here and go back in the morning? It's midnight, Gregory. It would be the most intelligent thing to do.'

He was so long replying that she began to wish she had not made the suggestion. Did he think she was trying to seduce him? The thought was ludicrous, but his continuing silence made it seem less so.

'I'm willing to take a chance on getting back if you are,' she said quickly, and put her hand on the door.

His large one covered it. 'Of course we'll stay,' he said in a strange voice. 'You're right; it's the wisest thing to do. Wait here while I fetch the cases from the car.'

Shrugging on his coat, he dashed out into the darkness. Within a moment he was back with the luggage and carrying it up the stairs. She followed him as he set her case in the bedroom at the back of the house.

'I'll be in the room facing,' he said, 'but I think you've got everything you need.'

'I'm sure I have. But I'll go down and wash up first.'

'Stay in your room,' he said roughly. 'Leave the damn plates!'

'But I——'

He closed the door on her as she was still talking, and with a tremulous sigh she went over to it and listened. His steps crossed the hall and then his own door closed. A tender smile curved her lips. Whoever would believe that Gregory Scott was shy with her?

Musing on this, she undressed. The bedroom was warmer than when she had come up here earlier and, touching the radiator, she found it to be hot. Gregory must have switched it on. Perhaps he had suspected they would be forced to stay here tonight but had been reluctant to tell her. If she had not suggested it herself he would no doubt have tried to drive up the lane. Once again she smiled. How furious he would have been if the car had stuck in the mud! She had not yet seen him lose his temper, but she was sure he had one. Slipping on her nightdress, she climbed into bed.

Outside, the wind howled and the rain beat a heavy

tattoo against the windows. She glanced at the door and saw the key in the lock. She felt no urge to turn it nor even the slightest apprehension that Gregory would come in. It was rather a pity that he wouldn't. It would at least have put an end to the will he, won't he, would she, wouldn't she, syndrome. Amused by this thought, she snuggled down and fell asleep.

CHAPTER NINE

PAULA opened her eyes and stared at the sun-washed ceiling. Perplexed, she sat up and, as memory stirred, her fear ebbed and she relaxed on the pillows. She was alone with Gregory in a cottage in the country. It was an exhilarating thought and it gave her the energy to jump out of bed and into a bath. The water was bubbling hot and she guessed Gregory was already up and had switched it on.

Going downstairs a half-hour later she saw she had guessed correctly, for the smell of bacon and eggs filled the living-room and Gregory, in slacks and a thick yellow sweater, was standing by the coffee percolator. She stood for a moment watching him, and only moved forward when he turned and saw her.

'Good morning,' she said huskily, inexplicably shy.

He came over and kissed the tip of her nose. 'For a tiger lily, you look fresh as a daisy.' He tweaked her hair and pushed the heavy strands back over her ear.

'You're always doing that,' she protested.

He leaned forward and kissed the pink lobe. 'That's why. Come and have breakfast. I hope you're hungry.'

'Starving!' She sat opposite him in the kitchen alcove.

'There are no morning papers to read,' he apologised. 'I suppose that sounds like heresy to you?'

'I'm delighted not to have to read the papers.' She suddenly remembered the article scheduled for tomorrow's *Recorder*, with pictures of Jack Rossiter taken during his student days at Cambridge. There had even been one of him with Gregory, but she had seen it and withdrawn it.

'I wish I didn't have to look at the *Recorder* either,' she muttered.

'No business talk,' he warned. 'We left London to get away from all that.'

'I know.' She looked at her plate, willing her appetite to return; unsuccessfully.

'Coffee?' Gregory asked, his voice easy.

She nodded but did not raise her eyes as he filled the cup. But when she did finally lift her head it was to find him staring into space, his expression as strained as her own thoughts.

He did not look as if his rest had refreshed him and she wondered if there was something troubling him. Perhaps he was too personally involved in Jack Rossiter's case to forget it, even after office hours. Paula bit back a sigh. If only she had met Gregory before the series had been planned! If she had known of his friendship with Rossiter she would have prevented Ron from writing about him.

Anger robbed her of appetite and she pushed away her plate. How could such a thought have entered her mind? Only a week ago she had told Gregory she never interfered in editorial policy, now here she was wishing that she had done so. But no matter how much she despised her weakness, she had to face it. Face the fact that she would do anything in her power to help the man she loved, even if it meant overruling her editors. Her father would have been horrified had he heard such heresy!

She rose and carried the crockery to the sink. 'Did you sleep well?' she asked above the rush of water.

'Fitfully.' Gregory's voice was so close that she glanced up from the suds and saw he had come to lean against the draining-board. 'What time do you want to leave?'

She piled the plates into the water and did not look at him. 'Are you in any particular rush?'

'No.'

'Then let's stay here till the afternoon. It looks as if it's going to be a lovely day.'

'Paula, I——'

She raised her head and said quickly: 'Don't apologise for mistaking the weekend. I'm enjoying myself here.'

'You are, aren't you?' he said in a strange voice, and turned towards the back door.

'Where are you going?'

'To get some logs. Tom keeps them in the shed at the bottom of the garden. I'll dig out a wheelbarrow and bring a stack in.'

She laughed, suddenly happy without knowing why. But of course she did know why. Hearing Gregory talk of bringing in some logs sounded so domestic that it took their relationship out of the delicate spun glass atmosphere of newspaper-tycoon-meets-dynamic-lawyer and into the homely reality of domesticity.

'I adore log fires,' she said. 'Even if it's warm during the day, we can light one this evening.'

'This evening?'

'Why not?' She was cool to the point of over-composure. 'If the weather keeps fine there's no reason why we can't stay here till tomorrow—if you're not scared of me, that is.'

Without answering, Gregory went out. Puzzled, she continued to wash up. She was stacking the dishes when she heard a key turn in the front door. Heart pounding, she peered through the kitchen window. Gregory was several hundred yards away and though she knocked on the pane he did not hear her. Hands hovering above a saucepan, she waited as the front door opened, and only relaxed as a dumpy woman bustled in.

'I didn't know you'd be up so early,' the visitor said, closing the door and trotting across the living-room. She

was in her fifties, with sharp features and pale grey eyes that
darted around like a ball in a pinball machine. 'I'm Mrs
Anderson,' she continued. 'Mr Scott not down yet?'

'He's collecting some logs.' Paula stacked some plates.
'How did you know Mr Scott was here?'

'I know his car.' The woman approached the sink. 'I'll
finish those for you. That's what I'm here for.'

Assuming Mrs Anderson to be the daily, Paula stepped
back and wiped her hands. 'It was an awful storm last
night,' she said, feeling an explanation for their presence
was necessary. 'Otherwise we wouldn't have stayed over.'

Detergent liquid bubbled and Mrs Anderson sneezed.
'Makes no difference to me what you do.'

'I'm sure it doesn't. I was just explaining why we stayed.
With Mr and Mrs Parish being away——'

'Their friends often use the cottage when they aren't
here. It's like this every winter.'

'Every winter?' Paula echoed.

'When the Parishes go off. They leave in December and
come back in April. Have done for the last five years. It's
on account of his job.'

Paula was not sure she had heard correctly. 'Did you
say the Parishes left in *December*?'

'That's right. A week before Christmas. Same as they
always do.' The woman bustled over to the cupboard. 'If
you'd like me to prepare your dinner tonight, I'd be happy
to oblige. You'd have to pay me, though. Mrs Parish only
pays me to come in and tidy up.'

'That won't be necessary, thank you,' Paula said with an
effort. 'We'll be leaving this afternoon.'

'No need to go on my account,' Mrs Anderson stated.
'City folks think country people are narrow-minded. Live
and let live, I say. So long as folk are kind and honest, I
don't care what else they do.' The pale eyes flickered to
Paula's ringless hands. 'You're not married, so you're not
cheating on a husband.'

Paula trembled and backed away. 'I'm not—Mr Scott

and I aren't. . . .' She swung round. 'Mr Scott and I are friends, nothing more.'

'No need to *be* anything more these days.' Mrs Anderson regarded Paula's beautifully cut trousers and the gold cashmere sweater that heightened the tawny flecks in her eyes. 'You look as if you're a model.'

'I'm not.'

'Funny. Your face seems familiar.'

Paula backed into the living-room, trying not to look as if she were running away. When her father had died and she had taken over the company, the newspapers had had a field day with her; since then, she was frequently recognised by strangers.

But Mrs Anderson no longer seemed curious, and was rummaging in a cupboard for a duster and Hoover. She was on her way towards the stairs when Gregory came in, his arms filled with logs. The daily beamed at him.

'I was just telling your girl-friend I'd be happy to cook dinner for you.'

'That won't be necessary,' he said, and though his voice was soft, there was something in the tone that stopped Mrs Anderson from saying any more.

She bustled up the stairs and Gregory set the logs in the grate and then straightened to look at Paula.

'You knew your friends were away,' she stated. 'You didn't mistake the week.'

'I was going to tell you.'

'Before or after you'd seduced me?'

'Don't be foolish. If I'd wanted to do that, I needn't have brought you here. My home was as good a place as any.'

Remembering his lovemaking there, she could not disagree.

'Then why the elaborate charade last night?' she asked. 'Calling your friends when we arrived and pretending surprise when they weren't here. What was it for?' His lips came together and she noticed how pale he was. 'Were you hoping I wouldn't find out you were lying? If Mrs Anderson hadn't arrived when she did, I'd never have known. You must have forgotten about her.'

'I didn't forget. I was counting on her coming. It was part of the plan.'

'What plan?'

He put his hands into the pockets of his trousers. It hunched his shoulders and made them look broader.

'What did Mrs Anderson say to you when she saw you?' he asked.

'What do you think?' Paula's voice trembled and she was annoyed for reacting like a teenager. Except that teenagers these days were a sight more sophisticated than she was.

'Well?' Gregory insisted.

'She assumed we were lovers and hastened to assure me she was very broad-minded.'

'Were you embarrassed?'

'I told her it wasn't true.'

'The facts made you look a liar.' Gregory took his hands from his trouser pockets and leaned against the chimney breast. 'Let's see it from Mrs Anderson's side. Her employers go away every winter and all their friends know it —which includes me. She comes in on a Saturday morning and finds you in the kitchen doing the dishes and me in the garden cutting the logs—a very domestic scene.'

'Two bedrooms have been used,' Paula said quickly.

'I made my bed before I came down,' he replied. 'And yours is a large double one.'

'So what? I'm only trying to work out why you lied to me. If you wanted to spend the weekend with me you should have said so.'

'I didn't try and seduce you, did I?'

'That makes it even more inexplicable.'

'Not when you know the facts. I brought you up here to prove a point.'

'I don't follow you. What point?'

'That facts can *lie*. Every single fact about our staying here indicates that we were lovers. But you and I know that isn't true.'

Paula was still unable to understand what he was trying to say. Had he taken her away for the weekend—brought her to this particular place simply to prove that facts could lie?

'Why, Gregory?'

'So that you could see for yourself how easy it is to misjudge other people.'

Her bewilderment gave way to horror. It cooled her skin and tingled her scalp; it laid dampness upon her breasts. The harshness in his voice reminded her of the time he had come to her office. Hard on this memory came other vivid ones: his avowal to make her regret her decision to continue the articles on Jack Rossiter; his fury when she had said her paper's evidence of the man's guilt was based on solid facts and Gregory's flat assertion that facts could lie. All too clearly she saw what he had done; understood the motivation for his behaviour.

'Do you believe that the end justifies any means?' she asked huskily.

'Any means should be used to prove a person's innocence.'

'Even if another innocent person is destroyed by it?'

'You can hardly say I've destroyed you. All I've done is shown you how easily a fact can be misinterpreted. Things are rarely what they seem. I tried to get you to see that two weeks ago, but you wouldn't listen to me, so I made up my mind to prove to you that you were wrong.'

'I was certainly wrong,' she agreed, and the anger she felt for him turned inwards, making her hate herself for believing in him; for having read something so different into his behaviour.

'Every action that Mr Smith saw as a sign of Jack's guilt

could equally have indicated his innocence.' Gregory was
speaking again, the words coming out fast, as if he wanted
to make his position clear before she could stop him.
'Smith condemns Jack for being stupid in not covering his
tracks. He can't believe that it's *because* Jack was innocent
that he let himself be made into the scapegoat.'

'Do you expect me to believe he was being used?' Paula
burst out.

'Yes, I do.'

'The way you used me?'

'The way I used you to prove my point.'

'You used me,' she reiterated, 'and I'll never forgive you
for it. I should have listened to what Guy said about
you.' Her anger was no longer for herself, but for him. It
was as burning as the passion she had felt the night before,
but there was no joy in it; only a deep desire to hurt.
'You'd do anything to win a case for a client, wouldn't you?
Maria Marten and the Red Barn has nothing on you! How
far were you prepared to go, Gregory? Would you have
gone to bed with me or would honour have kept you from
the final *coup de grâce*!'

'Paula, I——'

'But I was forgetting,' she cried. '*Not* going to bed with
me was the whole purpose of the exercise. What a joke!
If only I'd guessed it, I could have saved my girlish fears
and enjoyed the pretence!'

'Paula, stop it. I wasn't pretending all the time. You
know that.' He went towards her, but she side-stepped
him.

'Don't touch me,' she cried. 'You and your facts. You
couldn't even make me believe it was Sunday!'

His expression hardened. 'I'm fighting for a man's future,
Paula. I had no option. Your newspaper is destroying him.
Has already destroyed him, if I can't make you retract all
the lies you've printed.'

'They aren't lies. They're the truth, but you're too blind

to see it. Rossiter's your friend and you'll do anything to help him—you've already shown me that for a *fact*! If you go to such lengths for your clients, I shouldn't think any of them are found guilty.'

'I'm only interested in protecting the innocent.' Gregory's control was slipping and his eyes blazed. 'Would you have listened to me if I'd asked you to make your editor re-check his evidence? To go back over the hundreds of damn stupid facts he'd dug up in the last three months?'

'You didn't even try. When I wanted to talk about Rossiter, you wouldn't let me.'

'Because all you wanted was to show me you had no authority over your paper. I had to *prove* to you that Smith could be wrong.'

'So that's what you think you've done?' she laughed in his face. 'All you've proved to me is that no one can be trusted; that the more power a person wields, the more careful they have to be in giving their friendship. I won't make that mistake again, so at least I've something to thank you for. From now on I'll stick to the people in my own world.'

'The ones you control?'

'The ones whose loyalty I don't doubt. Men who won't kiss me on behalf of their clients!'

His jaw jutted forward as he clenched it. 'I kissed you because I wanted to. You know it. You're a beautiful woman and——'

'You're a handsome man.' She cut across him wildly. 'Handsome and sexy. I might well have gone to bed with you if you'd played your cards properly. I might even have been mistress number three if you hadn't wanted marriage!'

'Paula!' He reached out for her, but she backed towards the hall, clutching at the side of the archway for support. She was shaking so violently she was afraid he would see it.

'It's over, Gregory. If you came crawling to me on your knees, I'd never forgive you for the way you behaved!'

The door was directly behind her and she turned and wrenched it open. Gregory's car was parked by the gate and she ran towards it and climbed in, seeing it as a momentary refuge. The keys were in the ignition and the urge to escape took precedence over anything else. In a surge of fury she switched on the engine. It coughed into life and she swiftly released the brake. The wheels spun on the muddy surface, but the car began to move.

'Paula, where are you going?'

Gregory was running down the path, his black hair wild in the wind. Fear spurred her to further action. Her foot came down hard on the accelerator and the car jerked off the ground and shuddered along the rutted lane. Through the windscreen mirror she saw Gregory racing after her and she pressed the accelerator harder. The car skidded violently and its bonnet narrowly missed the hedgerow. She swung the wheel sharply to the left and muddy water splashed against the windscreen. She peered forward to see out, unwilling to waste time looking for the wipers in case Gregory caught up with her. Ahead of her there was a gap in the lane and beyond it the tarmac road.

Taking a second glance into the mirror, she saw that Gregory was gaining on her. He was only five yards away and decreasing it with every step.

'*Move*,' she begged the car, but the engine though powerful, was cold and it spluttered and wheezed. Boldly she pulled out the choke as far as it would go and the car leapt forward like a cougar, almost throwing her against the dashboard. Down the lane she careered towards the main road, afraid to slow down in case the engine stalled. Taking a chance that there was no traffic coming, she shot out into the road, swinging the car sharply into the side to keep it from any oncoming vehicles. Nothing was in sight. Sweat suddenly poured from her, trickling under her arms and beneath her breasts.

Making sure the brake was completely released, she accelerated again, and only as the speedometer touched fifty did she dare look into the rear mirror. Gregory was nowhere to be seen. The road behind her was as empty as the road ahead; as empty as her life was going to be from now on.

CHAPTER TEN

IT was two o'clock when Paula reached home. She was glad no one was expecting her and was able to go to her room without being seen by any servants. Bitterness had kept her from crying during the long drive back to London, but in her own surroundings and without the necessity to concentrate on driving a strange car along unfamiliar roads, she no longer had need of control and she flung herself on her bed in a fit of weeping such as she had not known since the day her father died.

At last, spent from emotion, she rested on the pillows and tried to think with some degree of logic. She was not only crying because of Gregory's deceit but her own naïveté for believing he had cared for her. Since her middle teens her father had constantly warned her that men would not see her for what she was, but for what she represented in terms of money and power.

'Even if they have plenty of their own,' he had said, 'they may still want more. In fact men of power are the most dangerous, for they might use yours to further their own ends.'

Yet despite her knowing this, it had not stopped her from falling in love with exactly the sort of man her father had warned her against. Her eyes welled with tears, but she fought them back. She had already cried too much over

Gregory Scott. No man was worth it. From now on she would never let anyone come close to her again.

Wearily she ran a bath, and only in the warm, scented water did she relax and gain a sense of perspective over the events of that morning.

How furious Gregory must have been when Mrs Anderson had turned up and put paid to his little game. How long had he intended to play it, and when had he originally planned to tell her his real purpose in taking her to the cottage? Later in the day perhaps, or would he have first encouraged her to spend Saturday night alone with him too? One night would surely have been enough for what he had set out to do, though no doubt a complete weekend would have been even better.

Bitterness filled her, followed by physical revulsion as she remembered his kisses and her response to them. How he must have laughed at her! Small wonder he had always been such an easy-going companion when he had taken her out. Bearing in mind the painful dénouement with which he had planned to end their association, it had probably been no hardship for him to give in to her. What a consummate actor he was!

Thinking of the Saturday they had enjoyed at Southend, followed by the leisurely Sunday spent quietly walking through Hyde Park and then resting in his flat, Paula was shattered to realise that everything Gregory had said and done had been a pretence. She had never believed anyone could put on an act so skilfully; certainly not a man of his temperament. Yet it was his very rigidity and determination that had given him the strength to plan and maintain such a perfect charade. No wonder he had never talked of their future or said he loved her! Only in this had he shown some integrity. What would he have said had she foolishly let him guess the extent to which she had been planning a life with him? Of course he knew she had been attracted to him—their lovemaking would have told him that—but he would never know she had seen him as the one man with whom she had wished to share her life.

Later in the afternoon, as she idly listened to some music, she tried to visualise what that life was going to be now. Her intention to sell the company—vague though it had been—must be firmly put aside. From now on Grayson Publications was going to occupy all of her time. It was not the solution she had wanted, but it was the best she could do in the circumstances. Unions and the other attendant problems of big business might aggravate her, but would not destroy her. Only love could do that.

The ringing of the telephone brought her out of her unhappy reverie. Afraid it was Gregory, she allowed the butler to answer it, and a moment later he came in to tell her it was Ron Smith.

'Sorry to disturb you, Miss Grayson,' he began as soon as she came on the line, 'but I thought you'd like to know that we've just heard that Rossiter has killed himself.'

Shock vibrated through Paula like an electric current.

'When?' she demanded. 'How?'

'He drove into a brick wall a couple of hours ago. It was a deliberate crash. He was on a dry straight road and there were no skid marks and no other vehicles. We had a reporter on the scene straight away and we've got some excellent shots. Too late for *us* to use them, but I passed them over to the *News* for tomorrow's edition.'

'Good. If you hear anything more, let me know.' She was about to put the phone down when she remembered something else. 'Did he leave a family?'

'A daughter of eighteen. His wife died years ago.' Ron Smith's voice quickened. 'His suicide shows we were right, of course. He wouldn't have killed himself otherwise.'

'People might say our accusations drove him to it.'

'If we hadn't made them, someone else would. He knew when he started that he ran the risk of being discovered.'

Paula thought about Ron Smith's remarks long after he

had made them. He was right when he said Rossiter's
suicide confirmed his guilt. She wondered how Gregory
would have behaved if the man had killed himself a couple
of weeks earlier. There would have been no reason for him
to have come and seen her, she thought bitterly. No
reason for him to have pretended he had been attracted
to her.

She paced the floor, too tense to relax again. What would
have happened if she and Gregory had met under normal
circumstances? That night at the opera, for instance, when
she had been so aware of him and he had seemed equally
aware of her; sufficiently so to go to the trouble of following
her and Guy to their car in order to gets its licence number.
Or had that been a lie too? Another part of the build-up to
the let-down? After all, it would have been easy for him to
have found out the number of Guy's car any time in the
past week. She sighed. She would never know the truth.
Not that it mattered. She and Gregory were finished and
she had no desire to see him again.

She was by the window when she remembered that
Gregory's car was parked outside her house. The last thing
she wanted was to have him come and collect it. But she
had given Frederick the weekend off and, after a short de-
liberation, she rang her office and asked for one of the
company chauffeurs to come and drive the car to Gregory's
flat. She knew her unexpected return home—to say nothing
of arriving in her escort's car—had caused considerable
gossip backstairs, but she was past caring what anyone
thought of her behaviour. Indeed she had never cared. It
was an attitude instilled in her by her father; as so many
of her attitudes were.

Thinking of him brought him vividly to mind. He would
have liked Gregory; have enjoyed his razor-sharp intelligence. Theirs would not have been an easy relationship—
they were both too dominant for that—but the sparks they
would have struck off one another would have been warm-

ing for them both. She sat on the settee, legs curled beneath her. It was Gregory's strength that had first attracted her to him. It might even have eventually repelled her. To play dutiful wife instead of dutiful daughter was not the way she envisaged her future.

But no, she wasn't being honest. Gregory had a forceful personality, but he would never have demanded the same deference from her that her father had done. Once again she relived the day they had spent at the seaside: the hours walking on the damp sand; the fun they had had at the fair; the laughter and the teasing. No, Gregory had never treated her as if she were a submissive female or a great tycoon. He had made her feel a girl who had missed out on fun. Which only went to prove how perceptive and cunning he was; for to give her fun—all those childish and amusing pleasures she had missed out on—had been the best way of ingratiating himself into her life.

On Monday morning the *Daily News* carried a front page picture of Jack Rossiter's car, a mangled heap of scrap crumpled against a high brick wall. It was a gruesome sight and Paula shuddered as she looked at it. Did his death mean that his case against them would be dropped or would Gregory still persist with it? Her knowledge of law was not sufficient to give her the answer, and to clarify the point, she telephoned Guy.

'He'll continue the case in the daughter's name,' he confirmed. 'An eighteen-year-old sobbing in the witness box will wring the withers of the jury!'

'It's harder to prove the innocence of a dead client,' she argued.

'What he's lost on the swings, he'll make up for on the roundabout. Especially if it's a shapely one.'

'Jurors aren't fools.'

'I'm not so sure. As you know, I've never been an advocate of the jury system. Still, don't worry about the case. It's *my* problem. That's what I'm here for.'

He paused, waiting for her to say something. She could not remember if she had told him she was going away for the weekend. Even if she hadn't, he had probably found it out for himself. He might even know that she had come back earlier than she had planned. Nothing she did with her life seemed to be a secret, she thought sourly, and though she knew Gregory was responsible for her mood, she gave Guy the backlash of it.

'As long as I'm the owner of Grayson's, I'm the one responsible for its problems,' she insisted.

'You can still share them with me.' He ignored her tone. 'Are you free to have dinner with me one night this week, Paula? It's a long while since I've seen you socially.'

Because she longed to refuse his invitation, she forced herself to accept. 'I'm free tonight.'

'Excellent.'

'Call me later if you get any further news.'

With a promise to do so, he rang off.

She did not hear from him during the rest of the day, nor did he let her know what time he was coming to collect her. But being a man of habit, she assumed he would remain one, and she was waiting for him at eight-thirty, when he arrived at the house.

If he was pleased that she had agreed to have dinner with him, he did not show it in any warmer way than usual, nor did he make any reference to Gregory. He acted as if nothing had changed between them, which was the best thing he could have done in the circumstances, and she awarded him full marks.

It was only when they had reached the coffee stage that she decided to mention Gregory herself, knowing that not to do so—in view of Jack Rossiter's death—would be a give-away of her feelings.

'You'll let me know the moment you hear from Gregory?' she asked.

'I told you I would.'

'He must be feeling bitter as well as angry.'

'I don't see why.'

'Rossiter was a close friend of his. I don't know how often they saw each other in recent years, but I think the ties went deep.'

'Deep enough to affect his judgment?' Guy asked.

'I doubt that.' She made herself look at him. 'Gregory isn't the type to let emotion rule his head.'

Guy sipped his coffee. 'I believe you went away with him for the weekend. Did you enjoy yourself?'

'I came back on Saturday.' Her voice mirrored his. 'Didn't your spies tell you?'

'No.' He set down his cup with a sharp clatter. 'I promised your father I would always take care of you. I'm sorry if you regard it as spying.'

'I'm a big girl, Guy. I don't need a wet nurse.'

A waiter hovered beside them, asking if they wished for any more to drink. The little flurry of question and answer eased the tension, and when he had moved away, Paula was able to speak with pseudo-ease.

'I don't think I'll be going out with Gregory any more. The novelty's worn off.'

'I'm glad he didn't last.'

Guy could not hide his delight, and instead of being irritated by it, Paula found she was pleased. Guy must be genuinely in love with her if he could not pretend to be casual.

'How do you know he didn't grow tired of *me*?' she asked.

'No man could grow tired of you. You're too vital and interesting.'

'Tell me more!'

'Don't play with me, Paula.'

He was unexpectedly sharp, but she knew she had deserved it. The knowledge that she was trying to blow up her ego with somebody else's breath was shaming. Guy loved her. She had no right to use him: not unless she intended to settle for second best and marry him. She tried to think of him as her husband and failed. The image of Gregory was still too strong.

To blur it, she forced herself into an animation she did not feel, and when he suggested they went to a discotheque, she agreed at once.

Held in Guy's arms, she could only think of Gregory, and was overwhelmed with longing for a sight of his hard, ruthless looking face. Guy seemed boyish by comparison. He moved her across the floor, not too far away from her yet not too close. Covertly she glanced at him. One day she might be able to marry him. The only certain thing was that she could not contemplate sharing her life with anyone else. Guy understood her and had known her father; this alone would serve as a reasonable basis for contentment, if not the happiness she had once imagined for herself.

'Have you thought anymore about selling out?' Guy asked suddenly.

The question was so different from her thoughts that she smiled. Who was it who had said that men were more romantic than women? More sexy, perhaps; but that was quite different.

'I've decided to carry on,' she replied. 'I might launch a few more magazines. That wouldn't require too much capital outlay.'

'Advertising them would.'

'I'd restrict it to our own papers.'

'I still don't think it's the right thing to do. It's far better to diversify and not put all your money into publishing. There are lots of other leisure industries we can consider.'

'I still fancy magazines. What about technical ones? With people working shorter hours, those are the kind that will do well.'

'They still require money. And we don't have enough

reserves to dip into them. That's one of the reasons an amalgamation is worth considering.'

'An amalgamation?' She was surprised. 'I thought you wanted me to sell out?'

'You say you won't sell. That's why I'm suggesting amalgamation. It's the next best thing. It would bring in the cash we need, plus the personnel.'

His last few words told her he had a company in mind, and she asked him which one.

'Roberson Printers. They're the biggest in the business and they're anxious to keep their presses fully occupied. They're prepared to amalgamate or to buy you out. You should give it some thought.'

'I will,' she promised. 'But don't rush me.'

'You're the boss,' he smiled.

'I wish I wasn't.'

'If you meant that, you'd give up work and retire!'

She laughed, wondering what he would say if he knew she had been prepared to do that for Gregory. What was he doing now and with whom? She would have given a great deal to know. He was too attractive to be without a woman for long. He might even have a regular girl-friend whom he had temporarily deserted in order to play his role with herself. The thought was so painful that she gasped, and Guy immediately led her back to their table.

'I shouldn't have kept you up so late,' he apologised. 'I'll take you home.'

He refused her offer of a nightcap but kissed her good-night with an unusual display of emotion. It was impossible for her to respond, but she was glad she could prevent herself from recoiling. It was amazing what a difference there was in a kiss—not only the action itself, but the response to it.

With Gregory she had been overwhelmed by desire. His look, the fleeting touch of his fingers on her skin had been enough to make her incapable of logical thought. With Guy it was different. She stood passive in his hold, aware of everything around her and coldly, rigidly, aware of him: his quickened breathing, his cool lips and their sudden hard pressure which she wanted to resist. She pushed him away and made herself look as wan as possible.

'I'm terribly tired, Guy. Do you mind....'

'I know,' he said contritely. 'Poor darling! I wish you'd let me take care of you. We could have such a wonderful life together.'

'Not now,' she pleaded, putting her fingers to his lips. 'Let things be for the moment. You're still the only person I rely on.'

'A guard dog who can dance!'

Her eyes crinkled with amusement. 'A loyal one, then. I don't know how I'd manage without you.'

'You'd find someone else,' he said with irony. 'Clever women always do.'

Paula mulled over Guy's comment when she was alone. It gave her a clear and not very pretty picture of the way he saw her: a woman able to take care of herself; who would always find people to help her. But what was wrong with that? She needed people and she had been taught the wisdom of buying the best possible advice. That was why she had Guy and others like him.

A sudden gust of rain battered the windows, reminding her of the night she had spent at the cottage. Gregory's silence since she had left him on Saturday had surprised her, for she had been convinced he would make an attempt to contact her, if only to make some kind of apologia. That he had not done so showed her how much her accusation had hurt him. She was glad. She wanted to hurt him; would like to hurt him more.

'Gregory!' she cried and, turning her face into the pillow, wept because he wasn't the man she had thought him to be.

The rest of the week was uneventful apart from a

threatened strike at their Manchester office, which was luckily averted. Afterwards, Paula saw it as the lull before the storm, but at the time she was not aware of it. Not that there was anything she could have done even if she had been prepared, and the blow, when it came, was the more painful because of its unexpectedness.

'Mr Smith and Mr Ardrey are here to see you.' It was Mrs Maxwell who banged the first drum. 'They say it's urgent.'

Knowing it must be, to bring them both here together without an appointment, she told Mrs Maxwell to send them in.

'Rossiter wasn't guilty,' Ron Smith said as he stepped into the room. 'It was his assistant.'

Paula was glad she was sitting down. 'You ... you ... you mean everything we accused him of was wrong?'

'We printed the truth—except that it wasn't Rossiter who was guilty. It was his second-in-command. The man who gave us some of the evidence in the first place.'

'My God!' she exploded. 'Didn't you think of that? It's the oldest trick in the book.'

'I know,' Ron Smith said wearily, 'but these things happen.'

'Not to us,' she said furiously. 'Not until now. You told me you'd double-checked everything. How was it you didn't check on your informant?'

'We did. We treble-checked the swine after Scott became involved! But even *I* can be fooled by forgeries. Mr Ardrey was too.'

Paula looked at Guy. He was pale but stoical and made no attempt to avoid her eyes.

'Ron has a point, Paula. My office saw and checked every piece of evidence the *Recorder* had against Rossiter. It was foolproof; the documents, the letters he signed, even a tape recording we had of him discussing a formula with someone at Weaver Brothers.' He flung out his hands. 'All faked!'

She was shattered. The implications of what she had learned poured through her like water through a broken dyke. This could cost them a fortune. It could cost them their good name. It had already cost Jack Rossiter his life. And me my only love, she thought bleakly.

'Scott will take us to the cleaners,' said Guy. 'He'll go for the biggest damages in legal history.'

'He'll get them,' she replied.

'I can just see the judge's summing-up,' Ron Smith sighed. 'All the usual guff about the press having too much freedom to destroy people's reputations. Our rivals will have a field day!'

'All the evidence showed Rossiter was guilty,' Paula said. 'We didn't make it up or exaggerate. Surely that's a point in our favour?'

'If he didn't have a daughter it wouldn't be so bad,' Ron replied. 'But the *Express* is running a big story about her. She's a pretty kid and she'll get a load of sympathy.'

'We must settle out of court,' Guy stated. 'Even if we have to pay more.' He looked at Paula. 'It will cost us less in the long run.'

'Trite but true,' she said bitterly. 'Gregory won't only want his pound of flesh, but the blood that goes with it.'

'The blood was Shylock's downfall.'

'It won't be Gregory's.'

The silence in the room was heavy. Then Guy looked at his watch. 'I'll go back to my office and call him. I'd like to get hold of him before he starts preparing fresh papers.'

He hurried out, but Ron Smith stayed where he was, pale and determined.

'Do you want my resignation?' he asked bluntly. 'If it weren't for me, we wouldn't be in this mess.'

'Don't talk like an ass. If the evidence could fool Guy, it could fool anyone.' Paula swivelled backwards and forwards in her chair, finding the rocking movement comforting: like a baby in the womb. 'We can all make a mistake,

Ron. The important thing is to not make a second one.'

The editor's smile was bleak and with a nod he went out, leaving Paula to acknowledge that what she had said applied equally well to herself.

CHAPTER ELEVEN

FROM the little knowledge Paula had of Gregory—and since learning of his real reasons for taking her out she was inclined to think she didn't know him at all—she doubted that he would drop his case against them. With an eighteen-year-old girl as beneficiary of the damages he would get, it seemed far more likely he would press harder for a trial.

Even before proof had been found of Rossiter's innocence, he had been confident of winning. Now he knew that the man had been framed, he must be certain to go for higher damages still, claiming not only loss of name but also of life. Guy's advice had to be taken—if Gregory would agree to it. Unless they reached a settlement, they would not only be faced with enormous damages, but such bad publicity that it would undoubtedly affect their sales.

Her forebodings intensified as the week progressed. It would have been hard enough to forget Gregory in the normal course of events, but with Rossiter's death on her mind, she found it impossible.

Friday found her steeped in gloom, her normal radiance dimmed, her eyes lacking sparkle. How much of it was caused by worry and how much by her personal sense of desolation, she did not know, though she was thankful that everyone around her could assume it to be due to Jack Rossiter's suicide.

At mid-morning Guy came to see her, and as soon as she saw his face she knew he had good news.

'Scott has agreed to settle. I've just come from seeing him.'

Relief flared, then dimmed. 'Why didn't you tell me? I've been thinking of nothing else for the past two days.'

'I wanted to wait until I was sure.' He half smiled. 'You're not like your father in one respect, Paula. He would have been on the phone to me every hour.'

'*He* only *talked* about delegating,' she said dryly. 'He taught me to actually do it!'

As she answered, she knew she was lying. In the ordinary course of events nothing would have stopped her from contacting Guy every day—every hour even—the way her father would have done. But her personal involvement with Gregory had made this impossible. It had been imperative for Guy to deal with the matter in a legal manner, something she would have been incapable of doing.

'How much will it cost us?' she asked.

'Two hundred thousand. Considering the circumstances, Scott was less demanding than I had anticipated.'

'He must have had a reason for it.' Paula marvelled that she could speak of him so calmly.

'I don't think he wanted Rossiter's daughter to face the agony of a court action.'

'Would she have been called to the stand?'

'Most definitely—if we'd defended. We would have tried to show that the evidence against him had been so strong that even his own daughter harboured doubts as to his innocence.'

Paula was startled. 'Did she?'

'I've no idea. But we'd have done our damnedest to show she did.'

'Lawyers!' Paula said in disgust, then smiled to take the sting out of the words.

But Guy still reacted to them. 'If a lawyer is clever enough to see all the angles he's called sharp. But if someone in industry does it, he ends up being called a tycoon!'

She could not help laughing. 'What makes you think we live in a just world?'

'My continuing naïveté!' Guy became serious again. 'Ron Smith has learned his lesson. We've got off lightly, considering.'

'Hardly lightly,' said Paula, thinking more of herself than of the paper. The emotional price she had had to pay far exceeded the cost in monetary terms. It was foolish to minimise the hurt she had suffered or to deny the effect it would have on her entire future. She had only known Gregory a short while, but so swiftly had she succumbed to him that it would be years before she forgot him.

Anger at her weakness sent her pacing the room once she was alone. To think that she, Paula Grayson, heart-whole for twenty-seven years, should have fallen so blindly in love that her intelligence had failed to warn her he might have an underlying motive for seeing her. How could she have believed she was the type to appeal to a man like Gregory? He needed to be the dominant partner; required his every whim to be obeyed. His admiration for her cleverness had been a pretence—how clearly she saw that now! Still, it had been a worthwhile game for him to play. Two hundred thousand pounds was not a sum to be treated lightly in any currency, and it would go a great way to cushioning the life of Jack Rossiter's daughter.

A picture of her own father came into her mind. Would she have considered two hundred thousand pounds sufficient recompense for his death? Could any amount of money have replaced him? The idea was so ludicrous that she realised how cynical her earlier thoughts had been.

With a deepening sense of remorse, Paula knew an urge to see Jack Rossiter's daughter and tell her how sorry she was. She reached for the telephone and then stopped. She could not talk to the girl in such an impersonal way. She had to face her and expiate her guilt for having caused a man to take his life. Because she *was* guilty: the way Ron

Smith was, and Guy. The way everyone was who had printed those articles without protest. Does the end justify the means? she had asked Gregory, when instead she should have been putting her own house in order. An increase in sales, no matter how important, was not more important than a human life! There was good reason behind the laws of libel and slander. From now on she would make sure none of her publications skirted around them, regardless of how safely they could do so.

But she still wanted to see Rossiter's daughter. Gregory was the only person who could effect an introduction: he was also the next person to whom she owed an apology. Had she listened to him and studied the facts he had wanted to give her about Rossiter, this whole tragedy might have been avoided.

Was she trying to find an excuse for the way he had behaved with her? No, that was definitely not true. He might have had justification for wanting to prove to her that facts could lie, but the way he had set about it had been despicable. To believe anything else was to pander to her feelings for him.

Yet the editors of her own papers thought otherwise and acted accordingly. Like Ron Smith had done. He hadn't cared whom he had harassed in order to get his story and he would do the same again if given the same opportunity And what would she do? The question was hard to answer, since she had prided herself on allowing her editors the freedom to run their papers the way they saw fit. Now she knew she could not go on doing so. As long as Grayson Publications was in her control, they would have to defer to her sense of right and wrong. It would mean arguments and possibly even resignations, but she was not going to be dissuaded from her course of action.

Having decided to see Gregory, Paula was able to put him out of her mind. Later this evening she would work out the best way of doing it; whether to telephone him or to write. But for the moment there was work to do.

With a relish she had not shown for days, she waded through the masses of figures on her desk, then dealt with her correspondence.

She lunched alone, which she liked to do when she had no engagements, and afterwards prepared the notes she would need to face Sir Redwin Dukes, chairman of an insurance company that held a large block of their shares. Although it was not sufficient to give them a director on her Board, it was large enough to command respect lest they sold their block to someone who already had a large holding. As Guy was constantly warning her, Grayson Publications was hers to control only so long as none of the shareholders pooled their strength. It meant she was continually walking a tightrope of diplomacy, but short of sell-ing out or buying more shares on the open market—which she did not want to do because of the vast sums of money involved—she had no option.

Half an hour before her meeting was due, Sir Redwin's secretary called to say he had been taken ill with 'flu. Without knowing why, Paula did not believe it and she tele-phoned Guy to say so. He was not in and she left a message for him to call her back, then debated whether to go home early or to get on with more work. The prospect of facing another pile of documents was depressing, and telling Mrs Maxwell she was leaving, she went down in her private lift.

'Home, Miss Grayson?' Frederick asked.

On the verge of saying yes, she changed her mind. 'I want to go and see Mr Scott. Ask Mrs Maxwell to give you his office address.'

The chauffeur used the car telephone. Listening to him, Paula was in two minds whether to countermand her order. But knowing her indecision was a sign of weakness, she blanked it out, and sat in nervous silence as they headed towards Lincoln's Inn.

The nearer they drew to Gregory's office, the more agitated she became. In normal circumstances, when she was proved wrong, she apologised for it. 'It's humbling to one's pride,' her father used to say. 'And as necessary to a person as grit is to a laying hen.' The memory of his words made her smile, and some of the tension inside her lessened. It wasn't that she was reluctant to apologise to Gregory, merely that she was afraid of giving herself away to him. He must never know she loved him. Never.

Gregory's office occupied the whole of a graceful Queen Anne house overlooking one of those unexpected patches of green still to be found in old London. The interior was modern, with a marble-floored hall, teak reception desk and bronze chandelier. She gave her name to a uniformed ex-serviceman, and within a moment an efficient-looking young woman came down the stairs to greet her.

'Mr Scott won't keep you long,' she said, and led Paula into a tastefully furnished waiting-room.

The gilt-framed mirror on one wall drew her like a magnet, and she pinched some colour into her pale cheeks and applied more lipstick. Her eyes glowed like amber, as did her hair, falling like heavy silk to her shoulders. It was far too glamorous a style for her, she decided irritably and, rummaging in her bag, found a large tortoiseshell slide which she had meant to give to Mrs Maxwell as a present. She caught her hair into it and fastened it on the nape of her neck. Unframed by softness, her face was starkly visible: the wide forehead and winging brows; the high cheekbones and the smooth curve going down to the firm lines of her chin.

The secretary returned and Paula followed her up the carpeted stairs to the first floor. A mahogany door opened and Paula entered a large room. Gregory was seated behind a desk at the far end, and he rose and came forward. His eyes met hers with a directness that held no trace of embarrassment. How dared he be so shameless! Anger leavened her nervousness and helped her to retain her composure.

'Forgive me for keeping you waiting,' he said formally, and held out a chair.

There was no expression on his face and she knew he was waiting for her to speak. Did he think she had come here to re-open their last angry confrontation? Whatever was in his mind, he had no intention of divulging it. Digging her hands into the pockets of her fur coat, she leaned back in the chair. She was unaware of the elegant picture she made; her heart-shaped face rising from a swathe of tawny fur, a few tendrils of hair curling softly against her ears.

'It seems we were wrong about Jack Rossiter.' Her voice was louder than she had intended and she lowered it. 'I came here to apologise. If I had taken things into my own hands—not relied on what my editor said—the whole tragedy would have been avoided.'

'You prided yourself on your policy of non-interference,' said Gregory.

'Well, I was wrong.'

'I'm glad you realise it.'

It was a statement; flat, concise, with no hint of 'I told you so' in it. But then he had no need to let his satisfaction show. Events spoke for themselves.

'I wanted to tell you this before,' she went on, 'but it seemed advisable to let Guy settle things first.'

'I wouldn't have taken advantage of your guilty conscience,' he said, with a first hint of exasperation.

She swallowed her anger. How dared he talk of not taking advantage of her when he had already done so?

'How ... how is Miss Rossiter?' she asked. 'I—I suppose she—she took it very badly?'

Gregory returned to his chair behind the desk, an indication that he knew her visit was a business one. 'Wouldn't you, in similar circumstances?'

'Of course. That's why I'm here.'

He gave her a surprised look and she hurried on, not giving herself any more time to think. 'I want you to tell her how sorry I am, how much I regret what has happened. If it's any consolation to her, you can tell her that from now on the policy of our group on these matters will be re-shaped.'

'You mean that, don't you?'

'I don't say things for effect,' she said coldly.

His mouth tightened. 'I didn't mean to imply that. But when one's been hit hard in the pocket, one often says things one later regrets.'

'I could understand that remark if I'd come here before we settled the case. Coming from you now. . . .' She jumped up, then paused, unwilling to walk out in anger. But she could not sit down again and she went to stand by the window.

'You're right,' he said abruptly. 'Please accept my apologies. But try to understand that I still feel angry at Jack's death—at the waste of it.'

'I know.' She looked away from him. But his image was painfully clear. He was wearing a formal black suit and plain white shirt, the same kind of clothes he had worn when he had come to her office. His lawyer's garb, she had thought at the time, and wished she had seen him like this more often. It might have helped her to remember the reason why they had met in the first place, and prevented her from dropping her defences with him.

'What is Miss Rossiter going to do?' she asked.

'She hasn't decided yet. The money will come in useful. Without it, she'd have had nothing.'

'Nothing?'

'Jack lived up to his income—such as it was. Scientists don't get the salaries you and I do. He had an insurance policy, but his suicide invalidated it.'

'If she invests the money we gave her——'

'Gave her?' Gregory flung her a look of fury. 'Is that

what you think you did? Gave her a couple of hundred
thousand as largesse from your sensitive womanly heart?
My God, are you so insensitive that you don't know what
she's suffered? It's bad enough when someone you love
dies, but when you know their death was unnecessary—
that it need never have happened——' He thumped his
desk. 'You're lucky you can write out your guilt by writing
a cheque!'

'If you think that. . . .' Paula shook with hurt. How he
must loathe her if he could believe such a thing! She continued, her voice shaking: 'But that doesn't mean I take
the blame for everything. The evidence my reporters found
against Mr Rossiter was strong enough to fool some important men at Scotland Yard. We didn't just dig up the
dirt and dish it out—as you imply. We checked and re-
checked and we brought in independent experts to confirm
what we found. If——'

'Don't make excuses for what your paper did,' Gregory
cut in. 'It's over and nothing can change it.'

'So it seems. You enjoy hating, don't you, Gregory? Is
it a necessary spur for your success?'

He did not answer and she gleaned nothing from his
expression. Moving away from the window, she went to the
door.

'If you don't wish to tell Miss Rossiter how deeply
sorry I am. . . .'

'I do. I will.' A chair scraped and she knew he had
risen. 'I'm sorry, Paula. I seem to be saying that too often—
but this time it's true. It was churlish of me to say what I
did. Of course you regret what's happened. We all do.'

She made herself turn. He was standing beside his desk.
The light from the window fell obliquely upon him,
sharpening the side of his cheekbone.

'I didn't behave so well myself,' he went on. 'I was so
determined to prove Jack's innocence that I tried to in-
volve you personally in the case. It was indefensible of me.'

Paula had not expected Gregory to apologise for what he had done, and she searched for some cutting reply. Before she could find one, he spoke again.

'If that damned daily hadn't arrived when she did, it wouldn't have been so unpleasant for you. If I'd been able to tell you myself why I'd brought you to the cottage. . . .'

'Stop worrying about it.' Paula found her tongue and her wits. She was not her father's daughter for nothing. 'In retrospect I found the weekend rather amusing. Hoist with one's own petard and all that.'

Gregory looked at a loss and aware of it, her confidence grew. Wrapping her fur coat more closely around her body, she gave him a model girl smile—that was for Mrs Anderson, who had thought her one—and said:

'After all, in normal circumstances I wouldn't have gone out with you. But *I was* trying to plead my cause too—or perhaps I should say the *Recorder*'s one—and getting to know you on a personal basis seemed the best way of doing it.' She saw the disbelief in his face and knew there was only one way to wipe it off. 'Guy wouldn't have let me go out with you otherwise, but in the circumstances it seemed the best thing to do.'

Gregory straightened. He did not move yet somehow managed to look menacing. 'Are you telling me that you and Ardrey——'

'Yes,' she interrupted, with exactly the right amusement in her voice. 'It's been an open secret for months.'

'You could have fooled me.'

'I was trying to,' she said with a laugh. 'And I did!'

Gregory went on looking at her, and determined not to let him take the advantage, she continued to lie.

'Guy was in my office when you called me—after you'd sent me those flowers—and he was the one who suggested I accepted your invitation to dinner.'

'Did he also suggest you should let me make love to you?'

'Hardly.' She gave him a brilliant smile. 'That was my own idea. I was afraid you might guess I was putting on an act—I'm not very good at that sort of thing—and I thought that if I let you kiss me. . . . You were always telling me I was nervous and shy of you, and I really did think you guessed my motives.'

'On the contrary,' he said softly. 'You fooled me completely.' His eyes narrowed. 'Did you fool Ardrey too?'

'What?'

'Does he know everything that happened between us?'

'Don't dramatise things,' she said with a shrug, and gained confidence from the darkening flush on his skin. 'We didn't do anything so terrible. Anyway, he likes to know that other men find me desirable.'

'I'd be happy to give him more proof,' Gregory replied, and came to stand directly in front of her.

More than ever, Paula was glad of her coat, for the thick fur hid the tremble of her body. Was this the first time that mink had been worn as an armour? She tried to see the funny side of the question, knowing that humour was her safety valve. Gregory was staring into her face, his own so near that she could see the faint shadow of stubble on his chin. She could visualise him shaving, standing in front of the mirror in shorts or pyjamas. Or nude. Yes, he was the sort of man who would enjoy the sight of his body. Women would too! She tried to blot out the picture but failed.

'Was it all an act?' he asked. 'All the time?'

One shake of her head, one touch of her hand on his would have given him the answer his masculine pride demanded. But her pride was stronger.

'It wasn't all pretence, Gregory.' Her lips were shaking so badly that she found it easier to control them by parting them in a wide smile. 'You're very attractive and an expert lover.'

'I was never quite that.'

'Luckily. That was something Guy *wouldn't* have been happy about!'

No remark could have been more calculated to hurt, and he caught her wrist. His hand went up her sleeves to touch the soft skin on her inner arm.

'Does Ardrey need to know everything?' he asked softly. 'We had some good times together, Paula. We can still have them.'

The urge to hit him was so strong that she could barely control it. What a swine he was, this man she still loved!

'It wouldn't be the same,' she replied. 'Now that you know the truth, it's taken away the fun. I enjoyed the pretence, Gregory, but without it....' Head tilted to one side, as if in contemplation, she eyed him. 'No, I don't think it would be the same.'

'You're a cool one.' He stepped back from her, dropping his hand from her arm. 'You and Ardrey make a good pair.'

'*We* think so,' she said.

His answer—which sounded more like an exclamation —was cut short by a buzzer ringing on his desk. He strode across the room and lifted the receiver. Paula tried not to listen, but it was impossible. He sounded angry and upset and when he finally replaced the telephone it was to stare at her in the same way.

'Now what the hell do I do?' he demanded.

'About what?'

'Jack's daughter. I'd arranged for her to stay with me for a few months until she'd got over the shock and had decided what to do. But her aunt's come on the scene and insists that Lizbeth go and stay with her in Manchester.'

'What's wrong with that?'

'Lizbeth can't stand her. Until the funeral, she hadn't seen her for years. Now she's become aware of her responsibilities and is insisting on fulfilling them. A niece with two hundred thousand pounds in the kitty is a different proposition from a penniless one.'

'Miss Rossiter isn't a minor,' Paula pointed out.

'She has to have a guardian for her money until she's twenty-three. That was part of the arrangement Ardrey made.'

'You agreed to it.'

'Only to make sure Lizbeth didn't get her hands on the capital until she was older. The interest alone is more than enough for her to have.'

'Who are her trustees?' asked Paula.

'Her father's bank and myself.'

'Then I can't see the problem. The aunt can't touch the money and she can't force her niece to live with her.'

'But she can make things extremely uncomfortable if Lizbeth stays with *me*.' His mouth narrowed in anger. 'She's threatening to report me to the Law Society for trying to exert undue influence over Lizbeth.'

'She'd never make that story stick.'

'Probably not. But she'd get a lot of mileage out of it. And I won't have Lizbeth subjected to any more publicity. She's had enough to last her a lifetime.'

'Can't she stay with some friends?'

'She doesn't want to. She's still raw with hurt and she wants to be left alone. Her friends are pitying and envious,' he added. 'It's a foul combination.' He thumped his hand on the desk. 'Lizbeth's screaming that she'll run away and hide, yet I daren't ignore the aunt's threat. If I do, I could——'

'Let her stay with me,' Paula interrupted.

'With *you*?'

'Why not? It's the least I can do. My house is big and she won't be in my way. I'll be happy for her to stay as long as she likes.'

'She might not like,' he said flatly.

There was no need for Paula to ask what he meant. Self-pity threatened to bring tears, and she blinked her lids rapidly.

'Don't make me into an ogre, Gregory. Jack Rossiter

was set up as a scapegoat long before my reporters came
on the scene. If we hadn't uncovered that phoney evidence,
someone else would have done so.'

'Is that more salving for your conscience?' he sneered.
'If the money you gave wasn't enough, you can always give
more!'

Bitterness threatened to choke her, but she swallowed it
down. 'I'm giving my home instead. It will be as painful
for me to see Rossiter's daughter as for her to see me. But
if you don't want it. . . .'

Paula was at the door when Gregory spoke her name.
She half turned and looked at him over her shoulder, knowing that if he made one more hurtful comment she
would want to kill him.

'I'll talk to her and see what she says,' he stated. 'If she
does agree to stay with you, it wouldn't have to be for long.
Once she's got over her grief, she'll be capable of making
a life for herself. I'll bring her round to you this evening,
if I may. If she agrees, that is.'

'Let me know if you aren't coming.'

He nodded. 'If you don't hear from me, we'll be with
you about nine.'

Paula nodded and went out. As she reached the top of
the stairs he caught up with her.

'I appreciate you coming to see me,' he said quietly. 'But
next time one of your newspapers is in trouble, don't put
yourself up as a sacrificial lamb. You might get cooked.'

'But never eaten, Gregory. I'm too tough! Don't bother
to see me out,' she added, and ran swiftly down the stairs.
Only as she reached the bottom step did she stumble and
tighten her hold on the banister. Then in command of herself again, she crossed the marble hall.

She saw the brass nameplate as she closed the door
behind her. Gregory Scott—Solicitor. Her mouth tightened. Philanderer and pretender was a more apt description.
If she remembered that, she might eventually be able to
forget him.

CHAPTER TWELVE

LIZBETH ROSSITER was a surprise. Expecting a young girl bowed down by grief, Paula found herself confronting a slim blonde creature with a doll-like face and a composed manner that made her seem older than her years. She wore black. New clothes, Paula noted, and expensive ones, chosen to show off the slender figure and porcelain colouring; not clothes chosen in a hurry by a grief-stricken girl.

'It's kind of you to let me stay here, Miss Grayson,' she said in a flute-like voice. 'Gregory says he's told you about my aunt?'

'Briefly.' Paula held out her hand. 'You're very welcome here, Lizbeth. I may call you that, mayn't I?'

The girl nodded and looked at Gregory who was setting her cases on the floor. Paula signalled the butler to take them and then led the way into the drawing-room.

'I never expected a house like this,' Lizbeth Rossiter said, and sounded so nervous that for the first time Paula warmed to her.

'You'll soon get used to its size. I never notice it.'

'How long have you lived here?'

'All my life. I was born in a room on the second floor.'

'Oh, I thought you'd. . . .'

Although she did not finish the thought, it was easy to guess what it had been.

'Did you think I started with a newspaper round?' Paula smiled. 'I'm afraid it wasn't that kind of success story. Though my father did begin by working in a newsagent's.'

The pale cheeks flushed and the small hands fluttered. 'I know all about your life, Miss Grayson. Gregory's already told me about you.'

'I hope you'll judge me for yourself!'

'I already have. Otherwise I wouldn't have agreed to

134

come here.' The limpid blue eyes examined Paula. 'I always like to make up my own mind about people, don't you?'

'I try, but it isn't always easy.'

'What about going to your room, Lizbeth?' Gregory intervened. 'You look tired.'

'I'm not a bit tired.' She went close to him. 'You must get out of the habit of treating me like a child. I'm not, you know.'

'You are to me.' He put a large hand on her head. A fine-spun thread of hair twined itself around his finger and he gave it a tug. 'Don't forget I first saw you in your cradle.'

'How *can* I forget it?' Lizbeth pouted. 'You never stop reminding me.'

'It's just my way of making sure you have respect for my age.'

'Pooh,' she said, and nestled against him.

Watching them, Paula felt as if she was an interloper. There was an intimacy between them that spoke of many happy years. From his manner it was obvious that Gregory regarded the girl paternally, but Paula knew instinctively that Lizbeth did not feel filial. There was too much guile in those big blue eyes; too studied an attitude in the way she played the little girl and at the same time told him she was a woman.

'I'll leave you to settle in,' said Gregory. 'I have another appointment.'

'When shall I see you?' Lizbeth asked.

'I'll telephone you tomorrow.'

'Will you take me out to dinner?'

He hesitated, then nodded before leaning forward to kiss her cheek. As he straightened, his eyes met Paula's. 'Thank you for coming to Lizbeth's rescue.'

Diplomatically Paula did not comment, and as the front door closed behind him, she turned briskly to the young guest who was still staring at it as though willing Gregory to return.

'Come on, Lizbeth, I'll show you to your room and leave you to settle.'

In a surprisingly short time, Lizbeth Rossiter made herself at home. She did not appear to have any friends—at least none she wanted to see or invite to visit her—and was content to spend much of her time listening to records or reading; pleasant occupations in themselves but hardly conducive towards helping her re-fashion her life. When Paula tried to encourage her to go out—by giving her tickets for various Press film shows or cocktail parties to which, as a Press baroness, she was all too frequently invited—the girl politely declined them and said she preferred to be alone. It was not the normal attitude of a young and pretty girl, and Paula felt it to be a false one. Lizbeth was putting on an act, though for what or whose purpose, it was difficult to tell.

She was no nearer to discovering this when a month had passed, for by then Lizbeth had made her own routine in the house. She spent the morning in her room listening to records or—if Janet's gossip could be relied upon—talking to herself in different voices. In the afternoon she spent an hour exercising in the garden, regardless of the weather, then retired to her room until Gregory called to take her out or, if she were staying in, until dinner was served. As a guest she was no trouble whatever; if anything she melted too much into the background, and many times Paula would put down the telephone or walk from one room to the other and suddenly come upon the slender figure, half hidden from view and looking like a lost ghost. Yet try though she did, Paula could not like her. She kept telling herself it had nothing to do with jealousy, but as she could not find any other valid reason, she had to admit it probably was.

'You're very welcome to invite any of your friends here,' she said for the fourth time in as many weeks, when she found herself on the way out to spend Sunday with Guy—

a normal occurrence since the arrival and departure of Gregory in her life—and realised that Lizbeth would be left in the house alone. 'You don't need to stay downstairs with them if you don't want to,' she added. 'There's a small sitting-room along the corridor from your bedroom, which you can have as your own. I meant to tell you about it before, but I forgot.'

'I'm quite happy with my own company,' Lizbeth said. 'There's no need for you to worry about me. Besides, Gregory's arriving back this evening and I'm going to meet him at the airport.'

Paula tried to steady the agitation that coursed through her at the mention of his name. Talk about a Pavlovian reaction!

'I'd forgotten he was away,' she lied. 'New York, wasn't it?'

'Atlanta,' came the correction. 'He likes it when I meet him. He says it gives him a feeling of homecoming.'

'Yes.... Well, I can understand that.'

Paula hurried out, trying not to think of the slender blonde girl waiting outside the Arrivals gate at Heathrow, ready to fling herself into Gregory's arms. But of course she could not help thinking of it, and Guy noticed her distrait manner at lunch and commented on it.

'I was wondering whether or not to give Ron Smith the go-ahead on the new series he wants to do,' she said by way of explanation. 'I'm not sure how popular it will be.'

'As long as it won't be litigious! But why not leave the decision to him? That's what he's paid for.'

'I still like to hold a watching brief.'

'Those words bring Gregory Scott to mind.' Guy was grim. 'How's the Rossiter girl coping with her new-found wealth?'

'I don't think she has it yet. Anyway, I couldn't ask her. Some things are too embarrassing.'

'I would have thought it embarrassing to have her stay

in your home. I'm still astonished that you did.'

'You know why.' Paula tilted her chin and gazed through the window at the green of Regent's Park.

Guy lived in the top half of a Nash house which his uncle owned, and which he had said he would buy if she agreed to marry him and did not wish to stay in Hamilton Grove. It was hard to see herself as mistress here. She sighed ruefully. Even more difficult to see herself as wife.

'Lizbeth's an odd girl,' she murmured. 'In some ways she's very young for her age—her boarding school education, I suppose—but in other ways she's far too mature.'

'Can one be too mature?'

'I think so. That's when it becomes calculated. I get the feeling she always does things for effect.'

'Most young people do. Especially girls. They can be devilish moody too. I remember my sister Jeanne—she drove us all crazy till she suddenly fell in love and got married.' Guy replenished their wine glasses. 'The trouble with you, Paula, is that you were an only child. You don't know how teenagers behave.'

'I was a teenager too—not so long ago. And don't give me that bit about the generation gap. I'm only nine years older than Lizbeth.'

'But years older in experience.' Pale blue eyes rested on her with studied appreciation. 'Anyway, you were never a teenager. You went from childhood to womanhood in one fell swoop!'

Remembering her father's eagerness to have her grow up and join him in the business, she had to agree with Guy. But only about herself; not about Lizbeth Rossiter. The girl was no ordinary, moody teenager.

Ten days later Lizbeth proved herself to be exactly that. In the intervening time she had only been in the house to sleep, having spent most of each day with Gregory, who was moving to a town house in Knightsbridge and seemed grateful for the girl's help. But having promised to take her out to dinner to celebrate the completion of the move, he rang through at the last moment to say he had been called to an urgent meeting in the City and would not be free to see her until too late.

She stormed into the drawing-room where Paula was relaxing after her own busy day, and defiantly poured herself a large whisky.

'He doesn't care how often he stands me up,' she said angrily. 'This is the second time in a week.'

'He's a highly successful lawyer,' Paula said, 'and very busy.'

'There are more important things in life than business.'

'Not to most men. And I doubt to Gregory.' Paula marvelled that she should be defending him.

'Gregory's different.' Lizbeth sniffed miserably. 'He's always found time for me before. When I was at school— miles away from London—he used to visit me every month. All the girls were so jealous of me. They'd have their boring old parents trotting down and I'd have this super-gorgeous man.'

'All the more reason for you to accept his excuses when he can't see you now.'

Paula was tart and could not help it. Blast the girl! Didn't she know how fortunate she was? This time her own jealousy was too obvious for her to ignore it. 'That's why I think you should start to cultivate friends of your own age,' she went on. 'You don't want Gregory to feel guilty because he can't see you, and——'

'That's exactly what I want!' There was no doubting the truth of Lizbeth's sentiment. 'I want him to feel responsible for me; to make me the whole of his life, not just part of it. I love him and I intend to marry him.'

Paula was shocked. She went to speak, found that her tongue was too dry and rubbed her lips together. 'I know you love Gregory,' she said. 'He's been part of your life for so long that——'

'Ever since I can remember. He's always been there.'

'That doesn't mean you love him in the way you'll love the man you want to marry. You're still so young.'

'And you're so old,' Lizbeth giggled, then looked alarmed by what she had said. 'I mean, you sound like Methuselah when you talk like that. I'm eighteen, you know. Mary had Jesus before she was my age!'

Paula gaped at her, but was quick to recover. 'Women have different opportunities these days. You'd be very foolish to get married until you've had a chance to do other things with your life.'

'Marriage isn't a prison. Anyway, I'll see much more of life with Gregory than I will on my own.' Lizbeth looked at her whisky as if surprised to see it. 'I don't know why I took this,' she said, and set it down beside the drinks tray. 'Gregory hates me to drink. He doesn't object to my having wine, but he never offers me anything else.'

Paula ignored all this. 'Did your father know how you felt about Gregory?'

'I doubt it. All my father thought about was his work. He never had much time for me. If I'd been clever scholastically he might have been different, but as it was. . . .' The narrow shoulders lifted. 'I wanted to go to drama school, but he refused to pay the fees. It's funny the way things have worked out.'

'Funny?'

'That he gave me in death what he wouldn't give me in life. Money,' she laughed. 'All the money I'll ever need. Isn't it wonderful!'

Paula looked away. She had suspected that Lizbeth had not genuinely mourned her father, but to have it confirmed in this heartless manner was more than she had bargained for. But it was not her business to comment on the girl's feelings towards her father, nor those she felt for Gregory either, now she came to think of it.

'I'll use some of the money to take a drama course,' Lizbeth went on. 'I feel in my bones I'll succeed.'

'You could be prejudiced!'

Lizbeth saw nothing funny in this remark. 'One has to have faith in oneself. Gregory calls it the power of positive thinking.'

'How original of him!'

This time the girl gave Paula a surprised glance. 'I don't expect you to understand how important it is to believe in your own ability. You never had to struggle for success. You inherited it.'

'I still worked in every department of the Group,' Paula retorted. 'And *my* father gave me no chance not to be scholastic. If I wasn't in the top four of my class each year, I had to swot away the holidays with a tutor.'

'Poor you. I suppose having a father who cares too much is as bad as having one who doesn't care enough. But at least I could turn to Gregory.'

'But don't confuse gratitude with love. Gregory is considerably older than you. He could be your father.'

'He's eighteen years older.' Lizbeth tossed back her hair. 'But mentally we're on the same wavelength.'

'That still shouldn't prevent you from going out with boys of your own age. Or at least in their twenties.'

'I have been out with them and I hate it. They're always on the grope! With Gregory I can relax and be myself. He's so—so devastating. He makes every other man look insignificant.'

Paula silently echoed the words, but aloud said: 'I think I'll give a party for you. Some of my directors have young families and I'm sure you'd like them.'

'No, thank you. I don't want you to go to any trouble for me.'

'It's no trouble. I'd enjoy it, actually. It's a long time since I gave a party. We have loads of young people working in the office too. Many of them have just come down from university and I'm sure they've got past the groping stage!'

'No,' the girl said sharply. 'It's too soon. My father's only been dead six weeks.'

With a shock Paula realised this was true. Yet it seemed so much longer since the tragedy had happened. Or was it because time now dragged heavily for her? The days were not too bad, but the evenings and weekends were unbearable, especially the evenings when Lizbeth was out with Gregory. Quickly she pushed the thought aside and rose.

'Let's have an early dinner and go to a film,' she said with a forced smile. 'An old maid and a young one!'

'Please don't be angry, Miss Grayson.'

'If I were ten years older, I might have been. As it is, I just saw your remark as childish.'

Happy to think that she had got the last word—better something than nothing—Paula led the way into the dining-room.

Paula found it impossible to dismiss the conversation with Lizbeth, and wondered whether Gregory had any idea of the romantic notions the girl harboured towards him. But he must have! He was too aware of himself not to know the impact he would make on a young and impressionable female. Look what he did to older ones! Or could his association with Lizbeth have blinded him to the fact that she was no longer a child? In normal circumstances Paula might have spoken to him about it, but she was very much on her guard with him and dared not do so.

He only called at the house infrequently and then merely to collect Lizbeth or to bring her home. He saw her at least twice during the week, as well as Saturday or Sunday —when he wasn't away for the weekend—and when he did go down to the country he made a habit of telephoning her before Sunday lunch.

Watching Lizbeth return to the table after one such call, a couple of weeks later, Paula could not help noticing her bubbling pleasure and remarked on it.

'Gregory's coming back early to take me out,' Lizbeth explained. 'He said he missed me.' She helped herself from the bowl of hothouse strawberries which was set in front of her, then covered them liberally with whipped cream. 'I'm getting spoiled living here. Out-of-season food and dear old Janet to take care of my clothes. I'll miss it all when I leave.'

'There's no reason for you to go,' Paula made herself say. 'You're welcome to stay here for as long as you like.'

'That's very kind of you, but I wouldn't feel free.' Lizbeth tossed back her long blonde hair.

'I could give you a self-contained apartment here. You'd be able to come and go as you want.' She hesitated. 'I'm sure that Gregory would prefer it.'

'No!' The blue eyes were bright and hard and the quick rise and fall of the small, pointed breasts indicated anger. 'Leave Gregory out of it. Where I live is up to *me*—not him. Can't you understand I don't want to go on staying here? If it hadn't been for you, my father wouldn't be dead!'

Dismayed by the anger she had unleashed upon herself, Paula acknowledged it was her own fault. Wouldn't she feel the same if she were in Lizbeth's position? Yet Lizbeth had not loved her father; she had practically said so. No, the girl's dislike of her came from other reasons. Jealousy; envy; a subconscious knowledge that in Paula she had a rival for Gregory's attentions.

'I'm sorry you feel so badly at having to stay here.' She spoke with composure. 'I suggest you tell Gregory.'

'He knows. But it was either living with you or my aunt—and anything would have been better than that! She's a real old goat! But she only decided to be a nanny goat when she heard about my money!' Lizbeth's temper had vanished as quickly as it had come and she was eating her strawberries and cream with gusto. 'There are several financial problems to settle before I can live the way I want. Our house was mortgaged, but it will still show a profit when it's sold, and Gregory's going to invest that for me too. But he says I'll have a regular income each year and he'll also let me have enough cash to buy myself a car and a small flat, as well as go to drama school.'

'I believe it's difficult to get in.'

'I've already been accepted.' Lizbeth's small mouth parted in a smile as she saw Paula's surprise. It showed her small teeth; sharp and small like those of a vixen. 'I've been having private drama lessons for more than a year. We had a daily housekeeper and I managed to get the money from her without letting my father know.'

'You were able to do a lot of things, weren't you, Lizbeth?'

'I managed to do what I wanted,' the girl said complacently. 'The main thing is to *know* what you want. Most people don't.'

Paula fell silent, shattered by this further insight into her young guest's character. She had never warmed to Lizbeth and the lengthening of their acquaintance had cooled it further. Lizbeth might be young in years, but she was old in determination. And she was determined to get Gregory. Paula set down her fork, all appetite gone. It was useless to warn him. He would laugh at her or think she was mad. Worse still, he might realise she was jealous.

'Have you started to look for a place of your own yet?'

Lizbeth shrugged, which could have meant anything. 'Does that mean you want me to go? I shouldn't have lost my temper and said what I did, but——'

'Forget it. I don't blame you for holding me responsible for your father's suicide.'

'Gregory does too,' said Lizbeth, helping herself to more strawberries and cream.

'I'd rather not discuss Gregory, if you don't mind.'

'Suits me.' Lizbeth went on eating. Her manners were precise, as was every gesture she made. Only in Gregory's presence did she become the little girl lost.

'What are you going to do with yourself this afternoon?' Paula asked.

'Nothing. Gregory will be back early.' Lizbeth eyed the remaining strawberries in the bowl, sighed regretfully and put down her spoon. 'I've promised to make him supper. Olive—that's his housekeeper—has gone off for the weekend, so I can enjoy myself in the kitchen.'

'Do you like cooking?' asked Paula.

'No. But Gregory likes to see me doing it. Sometimes he's a real sentimental old thing.'

'It isn't wise to put on an act with a man,' Paula said. 'You might be forced to continue it.'

'Gregory wouldn't force me to do anything. He's the easiest man in the world to manage.'

'Spoken with real experience,' Paula said dryly.

'You don't need experience to deal with a man,' Lizbeth stated. 'You need insight. I've known Gregory all my life and I understand everything about him.' A smile hovered over the small, full mouth. 'I think I'll make Spanish omelettes for tonight. Then I can get Gregory to dice the vegetables and beat the eggs. He loves to feel he's participating.'

Paula was hard pressed not to scream. All too clearly she could see the intimacy of the scene Lizbeth was painting. There was something demeaning in having Gregory described in this way; as if he were so easily manipulated by a selfish little brat still wet behind the ears. But it seemed he was being manipulated, and enjoying it too, if Lizbeth could be believed. Paula studied her, reminded of a Holbein portrait she had once seen. The sitter had been young and blonde too, with the same cool eyes and controlled expression that almost made one overlook the pouting lower lip, swollen as if with kisses. A fork clattered on a plate, and with a start of surprise, Paula saw it was her own.

'If Gregory's housekeeper is away,' she said, 'do you think it's wise to see him there?'

'I'm not afraid of Gregory. Do you think I should be?'

'Of course I don't. I was thinking of—of your aunt. She can still make trouble for you.'

'Not once all my money is invested and I have my own place to live. Gregory's told me that.' Lizbeth daintily wiped her mouth. 'He's never let me down and he never will.'

Paula's anger with the girl died. Behind the defiant words she saw the loneliness of a child who had felt herself unwanted. Small wonder that Gregory's kindness should have aroused love. That it was love born of dependence was useless to tell Lizbeth. She must find this out for herself.

'I know you think I'm a child,' the girl went on, 'but I can assure you I know my own mind. I love Gregory and I don't want to be with anyone else.'

'How do you know? You've never given yourself a chance to find out.'

'Why are you so concerned for me?' Lizbeth's anger, never far below the surface when she spoke to Paula, erupted with force. 'Or are you concerned for yourself? I've seen the way you look at him when he calls for me— like a cat at a bowl of cream!'

Paula made herself count to ten. Lizbeth was guessing; saying anything that came into her head that she thought would wound. I must keep cool, she warned herself. I'm dealing with a kitten. She's raking me with her claws, but she's only a kitten.

'I'm sorry you're so suspicious of my motives,' she said gently. 'But I assure you it's *your* welfare I'm concerned with, not my own. But since you feel the way you do, I won't say any more.'

'I knew you'd deny it.'

'That I'm interested in Gregory?' Paula laughed and ran a hand through her hair. She was wearing it loose today, and the gesture—with a tanned hand and gold bracelets on the slim wrist—had a sophistication of which she only became aware when she saw Lizbeth's look of envy. It was a pleasure to know the jealousy was not one-sided. 'He's an attractive man—I'll give you that,' she went on, then braced herself and went in for the kill, knowing that kindness wouldn't do it, and that she had to be crude. 'But he isn't tall enough for my liking. I don't get turned on by men if they're the same height as I am.'

Tight-lipped, Lizbeth pushed back her chair. 'I'll go to my room if you don't mind. I've some new records I want to play.'

Left alone with her Pyrrhic victory, Paula spent the next hour in the library reading a report she had asked Guy to prepare for her. Over the years they had acquired a great many offices, some bought directly by her father and some coming with the various small printing firms and trade magazines he had bought. Even when these had been amalgamated with other of their publications, or closed down if they were unprofitable, the property had been retained, becoming more valuable each year until, at the last reckoning, they had added a million pounds to the assets of the Group. Convinced they were worth more than this on today's market, she had ordered a revaluation, and it was this report she was now studying.

She sat over it a long time, but the figures did not make sense and she knew she was not concentrating. She shifted in her chair. The room was overly warm and dark, although it was not yet four. The book-lined walls absorbed the light and she was oppressed by the sight of the leather-bound volumes around her.

Picking up the folder, she went into the drawing-room. The long windows overlooked the garden, and beyond the leafless trees she saw the dense grey sky. She thought of Gregory at his house in the country and wished she had had a chance to see it. Immediately she was glad she hadn't.

It would have been another memory to add to the store she already had. How vivid those memories still were; each one jabbing at her like a thorn. My very own crown, she thought bitterly, and was not surprised when this thought took her straight to Lizbeth, who had likened herself to Mary.

The girl's entry made her look up with a start. She had changed into a purple wool dress edged with black. To make sure Gregory remembered she was mourning for her father, Paula thought uncharitably, and wished the colour didn't enhance the paleness of the silky blonde hair.

'Am I interrupting you, Paula?'

'It's a welcome one,' Paula said easily. 'I always find it tedious to work on a Sunday afternoon.'

'I can't imagine you not working. You're so business-orientated.'

'Don't believe the gossip columns! If I had the chance, I'd be a beachcomber with a paintbrush.'

'You're quite a good painter,' Lizbeth said seriously. 'Janet showed me some of your canvases. I'm surprised you don't have a proper studio. I'm sure you could sell your pictures if you wanted to.'

'Then it would cease to be a hobby. Besides, I only do it occasionally. It isn't something one can start and then leave. At least, if *I* leave it I never go back and finish it. And in the last three months, I've had so much work at the office that I haven't had the energy to paint.'

'You sound as if you're sorry you're a tycoon.'

'That's such a false word,' Paula said whimsically. 'It conjures up yachts and Rolls-Royces and chalets in Switzerland.'

'Is that untrue?'

'It should also conjure up loan stock and shareholders and unions and strikes!'

'And influence and privilege and power,' Lizbeth added.

Paula bit her lip. 'I'm sorry. I didn't mean to remind you of——'

'There'll always be something to remind me of what my father did,' Lizbeth cut in. 'It's a pity he took the easy way out and killed himself. He should have had the courage to fight you—which is what Gregory wanted him to do.'

'At the time, he didn't believe he could prove his innocence.'

'He should have had faith in Gregory—the way I have.'

The butler wheeled in a tea trolley and Paula signalled him to leave it. As she went to pour the tea she saw her fingers were smudged with ink from the notes she had made on the documents. 'I'll just have a quick wash, Lizbeth, but do pour yourself a cup.'

When she returned to the drawing-room her young guest was sitting on the rug by the fire, munching a scone. The delicately-boned frame gave no indication of the amount of food it absorbed and Paula was on the verge of making some teasing comment when she stopped. The mood between herself and her guest was not one to bear the weight of such familiarity. Instead she went to the windows and closed the curtains against the twilight.

'Isn't that the butler's job?' Lizbeth asked.

'I like to do it myself. Sometimes I prefer to watch the sky get dark and see the way the light changes.'

'You definitely have a painter's eye. You should——' Lizbeth stopped and she heard voices in the hall. Colour flowed into her cheeks and she jumped up.

'It's Gregory. He must have called for me.' Fleet as a gazelle, she ran to the door. 'I'm here!' she called happily, and flung herself against the tall figure that appeared on the threshold. Strong hands came out to steady her and Lizbeth's arms wound themselves around his neck.

Paula pretended to be busy at the curtains and heard Gregory's voice, deep but inaudible as he greeted the girl. Slowly she turned and saw he was standing by the fireplace, with Lizbeth still close beside him.

'Forgive me for calling on you without warning, Paula,' he said, 'but I made better time from Taplow than I thought I would, and it seemed silly for me not to collect Lizbeth on my way home.'

'You don't need to apologise for coming here.'

'I'll get my coat and be right back,' Lizbeth said breathlessly.

She ran out, and Gregory put his hands into the pockets of his trousers and stared intently at Paula. It was the first time they had been alone since the day she had gone to his office.

'You look tired,' he said abruptly.

'I've been working.'

He glanced at the thick folder on the settee. 'You should be busy with a husband and family. Not worrying yourself silly in a man's world.'

'That statement belongs in the Ark.'

He chuckled. 'I should have known better than to make such a stupid comment!' He moved forward, stopping as he saw her take a backward one. 'If I were Ardrey, I wouldn't let you work yourself into a frazzle for nothing.'

'Hardly for nothing,' she said dryly.

The movement of his head encompassed the elegant surroundings. 'Don't tell me you work in order to maintain this! You're a wealthy woman, Paula. You needn't do another thing for the rest of your life.'

'I didn't realise you were so knowledgeable about my affairs.'

'The fortune your father amassed was hardly a secret. Nor are the profits of your newspapers. Even the *Recorder* is in the black.'

'Have you been looking at our balance sheets?'

'Better than that,' he said easily. 'I've been made a director of Orian Press.'

Paula was barely able to hide her annoyance. Orian had been trying to take over her company for a year; no wonder he had acquainted himself with her financial position.

'I hadn't realised you wanted to go into business,' she said.

'I was asked to look after Orian's legal affairs from the tax angle,' he explained.

'Nor had I realised you were a tax expert.'

The narrowing of his eyes told her how dry her tone had been. 'There are many things you don't realise about me.'

She sat down, wishing she was wearing something more feminine than beige sweater and slacks. No wonder Gregory had said she looked tired. She had not put on any make-up nor had she combed her hair since this morning.

'You know that Orian are one of our biggest rivals?' she said.

'Everyone in the newspaper industry knows that. Also that they want to buy you out.'

'Is that another reason they want your expertise?'

'I don't owe Grayson Publications any allegiance,' he replied. 'I told you of my position at Orian because I wanted you to know.'

'Honest Gregory!'

'I know you find that hard to believe.'

The lines each side of his mouth looked more pronounced. She was not the only one who looked tired, she thought. There was a yellow tinge to his skin that came from deep fatigue and shadows beneath his eyes that spoke of more than a few restless nights. The vitality he exuded was only surface deep; when one looked at him closely one was aware of an inner exhaustion.

'You also work too hard,' she said bluntly. 'There's such a thing as the pot calling the kettle black.'

'I enjoy my work.'

'So do I.'

'But I think you'd be happy to give yours up,' he said.

'And do what?'

'Run a home, have children. If I were Ardrey, I'd find plenty of ways to occupy your mind and body.' He heard her gasp and gave a rueful smile. 'Sorry about that. It slipped out.'

'You're obsessed with sex,' she said tightly. 'It often signifies a desire to prove one's masculinity.'

He looked at her in astonishment, then threw back his head and laughed. It was such a vibrant sound that she wouldn't have been surprised if the glass chandelier had tinkled.

'You deserve top marks for trying, Paula, I'll say that for you. But I've no need to prove myself. And two mistresses in four years can hardly be called having an obsession with sex!'

'You've always had to have a woman,' she retorted.

'I'm managing without one at the moment,' he said quietly.

She looked away from him but knew she had to bring the conversation back to a lighter level.

'I'm sure there's a reason for your celibacy,' she said lightly.

'Love,' he said, his tone so much like hers that she was sure he was lying. 'I think I've become a romantic in my old age.'

'At least you don't pretend you're a teenager!' she commented wryly, then with a masochistic urge to hurt herself, added: 'Don't you think you should encourage Lizbeth to go out with boys nearer to her own age?'

Gregory's head lifted sharply and his jaw clenched. 'Lizbeth can't be judged by age alone. She never led the life of a normal teenager.'

'You know she wants to be an actress?'

'Yes.'

'Do you object?'

'Why should I? If she fails, it won't matter.'

'Failure always matters.'

'To someone like you, perhaps. Not to Lizbeth. She's different.'

'More feminine, I suppose.'

'That wasn't what I meant.' His eyebrows rose mockingly.

'If I didn't know your affections were otherwise engaged, I'd think you were jealous.'

'Since you know I'm not,' she said evenly, 'perhaps you'll give me credit for trying to do my best for Lizbeth.'

'That sounds as if you're leading up to something. What's on your mind, Paula?'

His direct question gave her the opportunity for a direct answer. But it wasn't as easy as she had thought; she still had to be careful not to let him guess her feelings for him. She frowned. What she felt for him had nothing to do with his relationship with Lizbeth. Had he been her brother, she would still have considered him too old for the girl.

'Lizbeth has all her life ahead of her,' Paula began. 'She's too young to think of marriage.'

'I didn't know she was.'

'You must know how she feels about you?'

'Oh, that.' He shrugged. 'She believes she's in love with me.'

'Aren't you disturbed by it?'

'I'm flattered I appeal to an eighteen-year-old.'

'That's pure conceit.'

'Most men are conceited,' he grinned, then seeing she was annoyed, stopped smiling. 'Don't worry about Lizbeth. I'll see she doesn't come to any harm.'

'Do you love her?' Paula asked, and the moment she spoke, bitterly regretted it. But Gregory took the question at face value, which gave her the comfort of knowing he did not doubt her relationship with Guy.

'I love her very much. I always have done. You've no need to worry about her.'

The object of their discussion came into the room. She had put on a short fur jacket and its collar framed her face. Her hair spilled like silver light around her shoulders and her eyes glowed blue as delphiniums as she moved close to Gregory and clung to his arm.

'I'm so glad you came back early,' she whispered.

'It wasn't just for you,' he teased, and touched her cheek with his finger as he led her to the door.

'Goodbye, Paula,' Lizbeth called. 'I'm not sure what time I'll be back, but I've got a key.'

'You'll be back before midnight,' Gregory added, and looked at Paula with such intensity that she had the impression he was trying to imply more than he had said. But as she sat alone in the drawing-room, she could not even begin to guess what it was. All she knew was that the sooner she had no need to see him, the better for her peace of mind.

CHAPTER THIRTEEN

ON the Stock Market there was a sharp rise in the shares of Grayson Publications and Paula was convinced that Orian Press was behind it, with Gregory Scott behind them. The thought was galling, made more so by the knowledge that her own company could do with his acumen. Guy had a good legal mind, but Gregory's was infinitely better.

As promised, he had brought Lizbeth back to the house before midnight on the Sunday evening and Paula, crossing the upstairs hall from her painting studio to her bedroom, had heard him chatting to the girl, and then Lizbeth's silvery laugh. She did not know if they kissed, but her imagination did not require any concrete evidence in order to visualise it. If he loved the girl, as he said, why didn't he openly declare his intentions and marry her?

On the following Wednesday she had her answer. The shares of her company hit an all-time high and the financial press re-asserted their belief that Orian were firmly set on buying control. Gregory's appointment as their new legal director came in for a good deal of comment, and she realised he would have been in an awkward position had his name been linked with a girl living in Paula Grayson's home.

What chance did he have of being happy with someone so much younger than himself? Lizbeth was no dumb teenager but a devious young woman with a subtle intelligence; however, in many respects she was immature, though this could well be an attraction rather than a deterrent to a man weary of sophistication. But how would such a marriage weather? The age group might not matter when it was eighteen and thirty-six, but it could be another story at thirty-two and fifty.

It was easy to imagine Gregory at that age. A lot less tense, of course—long established success would have seen to that—but just as virile and compelling as he was now. She ached to have his arms around her, to feel the pressure of his mouth. Furiously she reached for the telephone, not knowing whom to call but intent on calling someone if only to stop herself from thinking. Even as she touched the receiver, the bell rang. It was Morton Simmonds, chairman of the merchant bank that bore his name, and that owned a large block of Grayson shares.

'Are you free to see me?' he asked.

Since he never made such a request without several days' notice, she immediately agreed, knowing his reason had to be urgent.

He walked into her office half an hour later, a small, dapper man with a thatch of grey hair. After his usual affable greeting he came straight to the point.

'John Gower came to see me this morning—Chairman of Orian. He said they have sufficient shares to feel confident of succeeding if they make a take-over bid for you.'

Her heart started to hammer but she spoke coolly. 'They've tried once before and failed. What makes him think he'll succeed this time?'

'The fact that he's got the support of Marlow Insurance.'

It was her biggest shareholder and she made no attempt to hide the blow. 'How did he manage that?'

'By guaranteeing them a very high price for their shares once they got control. Now that Marlow has agreed, I don't see how we can fend off a bid.' Morton Simmonds pursed his lips. 'They offered *us* the same price, but we refused.'

'Don't tell me it was out of loyalty,' Paula said. 'I've yet to meet a banker who knows the meaning of the word!'

'I know you too well to feel insulted,' he smiled. 'But you're right, of course.'

'Then why didn't you accept?'

'Because I think the price will go even higher once Orian moves in.'

'How high?'

The figure he named shattered her, and she was silent for a while.

'Our shares will never be worth that much,' she said finally.

'They would be if the properties were hived off. They've been grossly under-valued.'

'No one else knows that. I only got the new valuation from Guy at the weekend.' She looked sharply at the banker. 'Even our own Board don't know the full extent of our property holdings.'

'Orian does. And they know their proper value too. John Gower as good as said so.'

Paula took a moment to recover. She had lived for a long time with the fear of a take-over and more than once in the last year would almost have welcomed it. How else would she get the chance to make a different life for herself; one more suited to her own needs and not those that her father had instilled in her? Yet loyalty to her father—who had built up the company with such love—had impelled her to fight off any attempt to acquire them. Now it looked as if the fight were over; won by means it nauseated her to contemplate. Which only went to show how naïve she still was in spite of being called the lady tycoon of Fleet Street.

'Who gave them the information?' she asked.

'Gower wouldn't say. He may not even know. The information could have been given to him by one of his directors.'

With the impact of a bullet, Gregory's name hit her. She tried to dismiss it, but it persisted, and she swivelled her chair round to stare with unseeing eyes at the street fourteen stories below. It was lighting-up time and the traffic moved along like illuminated ants, criss-crossing one another in a never-ending stream. How had Gregory managed to get the information and whom had he bribed?

Only a handful of people had seen the new figures: Guy; his private secretary who had made the photostat copies of it and who was as loyal as Mrs Maxwell, and Mrs Maxwell herself. None of them could have been bought. She would swear it. Swivelling round again, she met Morton's eyes. They were carefully veiled and she knew he was waiting for her to speak.

'I'll fight Orian,' she declared.

'You won't win. They have too many shares.'

'I'm not as pessimistic as you. If the small stockholders remain loyal to me, I can still keep control.'

'Don't count on their loyalty. I know you've been successful since you succeeded your father, but Orian have been even more so. Added to which they have first class management and a dynamic chairman.'

'What you mean,' Paula said bitterly, 'is that given the chance, the City prefers to back a man rather than a woman!'

'I'm afraid so. Don't tell me it's unfair,' he said quickly. 'My grandmother was a suffragette and my wife won't wear a wedding ring unless I do, and insists on being addressed as Ms instead of Mrs! But we have to deal with the position

as it *is*, not as we would like it to be, and my advice is for
you to accept Orian's offer.'

'You mean sell out my holding?'

'Not necessarily. But enough to give Orian complete
control.'

'Would you stand by me if I tried to fight?'

'Yes. I watched your father build up this business, and
if you want to carry it on, I'll back you all the way, even
though I think you'll eventually lose.'

Her eyes moistened and she hurriedly lowered her lids.
Not for the world would she let him see such feminine behaviour.

'Thank you, Morton. I'm ... I appreciate your loyalty.
But I won't fight unless I know I can win.' She pushed
her hair away from her face. Her amber eyes were dark
with the anger of her thoughts. 'Leave me to think it over,
Morton. I'll be in touch with you some time tomorrow.'

The moment he left she went to Guy's office. Only rarely
did she call on him and never without warning. He knew at
once that something was wrong.

'Morton's been to see me,' she said. 'Orian have the
new figures on our property.'

Guy paled. 'How do you know?'

'Their Chairman as good as said so. The only thing he
didn't disclose was how he got it.' She leaned against the
door, too overwrought to sit down. 'Who else beside you
and your secretary saw that report?'

'No one.'

'Somebody did,' she persisted. 'What about the sur-
veyor?'

'We used three different firms—the top people in each
one—to make sure they'd each only know part of the
picture. The whole thing wasn't collated until all the
reports were sent to me.' He looked faintly put out. 'But
you know this yourself. You were the one who planned how
we should do it.'

'I just wanted to make sure my instructions had been carried out.' Angrily she paced the room, her full skirt swirling around her long legs, her body quivering like a reed. 'Someone leaked that information and I intend to find out who!'

'Even if Orian hadn't got the new figures, they'd still have been able to make a pretty accurate guess as to what the properties are worth.'

'There's a world of difference between guessing and knowing. It was because they *knew*, that they were able to swing Marlow Insurance their way.'

'So they've got Marlow.' Guy pursed his lips and looked resigned. 'What are they offering for the shares?'

She told him and he looked even more resigned.

'It's a generous bid, Paula.'

'You want me to accept it, don't you?'

'We need to expand. And to do that, we need more capital and more management.'

'We could sell some of the properties. That was why we did the revaluation.'

'We need management too. There's strength in size. Honestly, Paula, I don't see why you're so against the idea. If it were your father, I could understand it, but. . . .' He hesitated, then decided to plunge on. 'If Orian comes in, the value of your holding would be trebled in a couple of years.'

'So would yours.'

'So could mine,' he agreed. 'And that's what business is all about—being successful.'

'In monetary terms.'

'What else?'

It was not the answer she herself would have given, nor her father either, and it made her realise with bitter clarity, how alone she was. Guy was a product of the modern breed of businessmen: investing capital to give the greatest return; seeing a company in asset value only, with no thought to the people it employed or the tradition from which it stemmed. To be a success today, one had to be expedient. Without a word she turned on her heel and walked out.

'Paula!' He came striding after her down the corridor. 'What are you going to do?'

'See Gregory.'

'*What!*'

'I think he's the one who gave Orian those figures.'

Guy looked astounded. 'What proof do you have? I don't like the man—you know that—but you can't rush off and accuse him of——'

'I damn well can! I have all the proof I need. I took the report home with me last weekend and left it in the library. Lizbeth was in there using my video machine and must have seen it. Once before I found her looking through some of my papers, but it never entered my head she'd actually open a briefcase.'

'Why didn't you lock it?' Guy was irritated and showed it, which he rarely did with Paula.

'Because I'm not used to locking up things in my own home. All the servants have been with me for years and I don't expect my guests to spy on me!'

'Miss Rossiter's hardly a guest. She's Jack Rossiter's daughter and you should have known what to expect.'

'Jack Rossiter was innocent.' Paula stopped walking and faced Guy, her own irritation matching his. 'If he'd been guilty, I wouldn't have had Lizbeth in my home.'

'I still can't fathom why you did. I'd have thought the damages we paid her absolved you from personal commitment.'

'Oh, Guy!' Paula's exasperation increased. 'Do you honestly think money can solve everything?'

He did not reply at once, and when he did he had himself under control. 'On your own admission you've just told me you think she read a confidential report and passed on the information to Scott. If that isn't a chip off the old block, I don't know what is.'

'She passed on the information because she's in *love* with Gregory. It has nothing to do with whose daughter she is. And don't smear Rossiter again,' she added icily.

'Sorry.' Guy dismissed the man from his mind. 'But are you sure she took the information to Scott?'

'Sure enough to ask him. He went away for the weekend but came back early. I think he did that because she told him she had something important to show him.'

'She must have known you'd find out.'

'She wouldn't care. She has no conscience and no scruples about doing what she feels is best for herself.'

'What about Scott? Wouldn't he know you'd guess?'

Paula braced her shoulders. 'It seems he didn't care either.'

'Then they're well suited to each other.' Guy regarded her with unusual gentleness. 'Do you think it's wise to confront him? Why upset yourself any more? He'll only laugh in your face.'

'I don't care. I still want to tell him what I think of him. Him and his integrity! He's nothing but a common thief.'

'It was the girl,' said Guy. 'If she gave him the information——'

'He didn't have to use it, did he?' She started to walk again, fast.

'Don't go and see him,' Guy pleaded, keeping in step with her. 'You won't alter what's happened and——'

'I'm going,' she cut in. 'Leave me alone, Guy. I'm not a child and I know what I have to do.'

Paula only stayed in her office long enough for Mrs Maxwell to ascertain that Gregory was in his, then she went down to her car and was soon being driven across the City.

Gregory was waiting for her at the door of his office, his expression impassive, though he must have been curious to know what had caused her precipitate arrival. As soon as they were alone, she told him.

He heard her out in silence, only the glitter in his eyes

and the swift way he retreated to stand behind his desk were evidence of his anger.

'Have you quite finished?' he asked when, her fury having exploded, she leaned exhausted against a chair.

'Isn't it enough?' she said wearily.

'Enough to last me a lifetime. I've taken more insults from you than. . . .'

'Don't pretend you're innocent?' Her anger flared again. 'No wonder you were so ready to let your lady love stay in my house! Did you give her a note of what to look for, or did you rely on her judgment?'

'Be careful what you say, Paula.' Red stained his cheeks. 'I've never slapped a woman yet, but there's always a first time.'

'Don't play the outraged innocent with me! You wanted to show Orian how clever you were, and what better way than by giving them secret information.'

'Orian didn't get the figures from me.'

'Pull the other one!' she said bitterly. 'Lizbeth was alone with that report for most of Saturday. She had ample time to make notes of what she saw and she passed them on to you. Why deny it?' she cried.

'Why indeed? You still haven't forgiven me for that weekend in Suffolk, have you? No matter what I say, you'll still believe the worst of me.'

'Does it surprise you?'

'Yes.' He looked grim. 'You were putting on an act too, remember? So why be so high and mighty towards *me*?'

His comment acted like a brake on her anger, warning her to be careful what she said. She had come here to tell him what she thought of him for using confidential information; not to hark back to the past.

'If I was thinking of that weekend,' she said sarcastically, 'it was because your behaviour with Lizbeth reminded me of it. Or is your show of affection genuine this time?'

'I would never ask Lizbeth to do anything underhand. You may believe that or not. I don't give a damn.'

She swung away from him, wishing she had taken Guy's advice and not come here. It had achieved nothing. Even the satisfaction of telling him how much she despised him had been less than she had expected, no doubt because the sight of him made her long to throw herself into his arms. She needed someone to lean on. She was tired of having to be strong.

'Paula!' Gregory's voice stopped her at the door. 'What are you going to do about Orian's offer?'

She turned round, hands in the pockets of her mink coat, head high and tawny hair cascading on to the glossy fur. 'I'll accept it and retire. I've had enough dealings with men to last me a lifetime!'

'Don't say that,' he said sharply. 'Accept Orian's offer because it's a good one and will revitalise your company. Not because you're feeling womanish and weepy and sorry for yourself.'

Her mouth snapped shut. Womanish and weepy, was she?

'One day,' she said, 'there'll be sufficient women in industry to make sure it's run without spying and cheating and lying. Until that time comes, I'll stay at home.'

'To cook?'

She ignored the gleam in his eyes. 'To paint pictures and concentrate on living.'

'With Ardrey?'

'Yes.'

Her fingers were on the door handle when strong ones overlapped them. Their touch was like fire and she pulled back her hand instantly.

'Are you sure your future is with Guy Ardrey?' he demanded.

'It's the only thing I *am* sure about. But don't worry, Gregory, I won't expect you to dance at my wedding.'

'Pity,' he murmured. 'I was hoping you'd dance at mine.'

Not pausing to answer, she went swiftly down to the waiting car. Huddled in the back, she gave way to the tears she had been controlling for most of the afternoon. Tears of temper and frustration, of impotent rage and bitterness. Womanly tears; which would have pleased Gregory if he could have seen them.

CHAPTER FOURTEEN

DRIVING home in the evening, Paula debated the best way of asking Lizbeth to leave, and finally decided to say nothing. If the girl had so little conscience that she could remain with her, then she would play her at her own game. Lizbeth Rossiter was not the only female who could act a part.

It was only when she went into the dining-room and found the girl already there, waiting for her, that she wondered if Gregory had said something to her. But the limpid eyes held innocence as they met Paula's, as did her conversation.

'The six o'clock News said something about your company being bought out,' she remarked as they sat down.

'Really? I was too busy to listen.'

'You don't need to. You make the news—why bother to hear it? Is it true, though?'

Paula picked up her fork and speared a scallop. 'The answer usually given in these circumstances is "no comment".'

Lizbeth smiled. 'Always the business woman! I was telling Gregory only yesterday how single-minded you are. He said it was because you'd been brought up that way. It must be nice having a father who sees you as his heir and treats you accordingly.'

Paula eyed her coldly. 'How did your father treat *you*?'

'As if I wasn't there. We each lived our own life. If we ever quarrelled, I'd get Gregory to take my part.' The small mouth curved. 'He always did, you know. Ever since I was a child he's been wonderful to me. I'm sure that's why he never married. He was waiting until I grew up. I don't think he realised it consciously, though.'

Doggedly Paula went on eating, wishing the fish did not taste as if it were plastic.

'This fish is awfully good,' Lizbeth commented.

Her comment was so apposite to Paula's thought that she laughed.

'Isn't it?' Lizbeth asked suspiciously.

'Oh yes, very good.'

'I'll miss the food when I leave here.'

Paula looked up. 'You sound as if your departure's imminent.'

'I'm leaving tomorrow.'

'Tomorrow?' Was guilt the spur or had Gregory been the one to insist? 'I thought you wanted to wait until your money had been invested, and your aunt——'

'She's no threat any more. Gregory suggested I gave her a nice present and she's accepted it.'

'That was clever of him.'

'He's very clever.' Lizbeth waited while their plates were removed and others set before them. 'He rang me this afternoon and said he's found a suitable apartment for me, that I can share with a cousin of his secretary's. Isn't that great?'

'Great,' Paula echoed.

'It means he can come to the flat and see me without worrying about anyone gossiping,' Lizbeth went on. 'Though I don't think I'll be living there for long.' She began to demolish her veal cutlet in brandy and cream sauce with the same relish with which she was anticipating her future. 'Gregory isn't a boy and it's crazy for us not to be married as soon as we can.'

'Are you abandoning the idea of a career?' asked Paula.

'Only temporarily. I wouldn't want to work for the first year. I'll be happy just to be with Gregory.' The blue eyes grew hazy with memories. 'He was so wonderful last night. I never knew love could be like that.' She gave a husky laugh, soft with embarrassment. 'I suppose you must think me very childish, but I'd never ... until Gregory....'

'Why should that be childish? I think it's eminently sensible to—to wait until you know you're in love.'

'I can't understand why you aren't married,' Lizbeth said with a youthful candour that did not dispel Paula's belief that the remark was meant to hurt. 'I know you're frightfully rich and successful, but——'

'There are no buts in my life,' Paula said crisply. 'I'm very happy the way I am.'

'Gregory said he thought you'd marry Mr Ardrey.'

Paula chewed her veal with the enthusiasm she would have shown towards bubble gum. 'Eventually I will.'

'When you've sold out to Orian?'

The question was so pat that it gave the lie to Lizbeth's earlier show of ignorance about the affairs of the take-over.

'Probably.'

'I'd recommend it,' Lizbeth giggled. 'Very much so.'

Not surprisingly, Paula slept badly that night, and as dawn greyed the sky, she bathed and dressed. The day ahead promised to be a busy one; there was a meeting with her own Board of Directors which was likely to last the entire morning, and in the afternoon she was meeting John Gower of Orian. If everything went as she anticipated, this evening would find her a free agent for the first time in her life.

The idea should have been exhilarating, but all she could think of was Gregory. Lying, deceitful Gregory. Anger seared her like a flame. But the burning did not cauterise and cleanse: it scoured and abraded, making her raw with hurt.

It was not the best frame of mind in which to meet her fellow directors and the session was a stormy one. To her surprise, several of them expressed their willingness to fight Orian, even though their own shares would be worth less if they won, but though moved by their loyalty, she refused to do so.

'Your father wouldn't have given in so easily,' Joseph Burroughs said. He had been on the Board longer than any other director and, as such, felt it gave him the privilege to speak his mind at all times. It was a privilege he rarely abused and Paula wished he had not decided to do so now.

'If my father were here, the offer probably wouldn't have come,' she replied. 'But we're living in difficult times, Joe. Only the big conglomerates can withstand all the financial storms. The small ones either fall by the way or amalgamate.'

'Then why don't we amalgamate with some other smaller companies?' the old man persisted.

'Because small companies in our industry are all under-capitalised.'

'*We're* showing healthy profits.'

'They're small compared with the money we have invested.'

'We'd get eight million for the property alone.' Joseph Burroughs glanced around the long table. 'That's why Orian want us. They'll take us over, sell the properties and amalgamate our newspapers with theirs.'

'If I don't get a guarantee that Graysons Publications will continue the way it is—give or take a few redundancies,' Paula said, 'I'll fight them every inch of the way.'

'Of course Orian will continue to run the papers,' Guy interposed. 'If there was so much as a smell that they

weren't they'd have the Government down on their necks
—to say nothing of the unions!'

'I still say let's fight,' Joseph Burroughs said.

'No,' Paula replied, and taking control of the meeting
drew it to a close.

It would be the last one she would chair; the knowledge
was saddening and she could almost feel her father's presence. But she must not think of the past. She had to think
of the welfare of the company and its employees.

'You've done the wisest thing, Paula,' Guy said when
he was finally alone with her. 'Will you stay on as Managing
Director if Orian ask you?'

'Never.' Her tone brooked no argument.

'Then how about us? You know I love you. How much
longer do I have to wait?'

He frowned. 'Have you fallen in love with someone
else?'

She forced a smile. 'You know the extent of my social
life, Guy.'

'It isn't still Scott, is it? I had a feeling he got more
under your skin than you were willing to admit.'

Her laugh was worthy of an Academy Award. 'Do
you think I could love a man I despise?'

'Women often do.'

'Not this woman.'

'That's what I wanted to hear.'

He bent his head and placed his mouth on hers. It was
as firm and dry as his voice and she remained unmoved by
it. He did not notice her lack of response and pulled her
into his arms. His kisses grew more passionate. His lips
were no longer dry and he moved them backwards and
forwards across hers, leaving a trail of moisture that she
could not bear. Putting her hands against his chest, she
pushed him away. For an instant he resisted, then he
stepped back.

'I love you,' he said thickly. 'Stop playing with me,

Paula. I've wanted you for years and you know it. Marry me.'

'No,' she whispered. 'I can't.'

His mouth trembled and he looked like a boy about to cry. Pity almost made her say she would think about it, but she steeled herself to keep silent, knowing she did not feel enough pity to sacrifice herself.

'I should have known better than to ask you today,' he said. 'You've had a difficult meeting and you've another one ahead of you.'

'It has nothing to do with that. I'm sorry, Guy, but I don't love you and I can't marry you.'

'We'll talk about it later. I'll come round and see you this evening.'

'No.' She went behind her desk. 'It was wrong of me to let you go on hoping. My only excuse is that I didn't think you cared quite so much.'

'I've always told you I loved you.'

'I saw it as more of a compliment to my ability.'

'I love that too.' He hovered by the door. 'I won't take no for an answer. I've known you too many years to give up now.'

Paula sat down. To ignore what Guy said would be to deny her knowledge of him. He was nothing if not tenacious and she could not face the prospect of having him as a persistent suitor.

'Most women would be flattered at the thought of perpetual courtship,' she said, 'but I see it as a nuisance and——' here she decided to be cruel to be kind—'and a bore. If you go on with it, you'll force me to stop regarding you as a friend.'

Momentarily his eyes closed. The bluish lids made him look vulnerable and again pity tugged at her. Then he opened his eyes and was once more the Guy of old.

'Very well, Paula. But I want you to remember how I feel about you. If you should change your mind....'

He went out, and Mrs Maxwell, coming in a moment later, was perturbed to find Paula leaning on the desk, her head in her hands.

'Are you ill, Miss Grayson?'

With a start, Paula sat up. 'No. Just relaxing.'

'How did the Board Meeting go?'

'It's all over bar the shouting. I should have sold out to Orian last year and saved myself twelve months' work.' And also saved myself from meeting Gregory, she thought, but did not utter it.

'You're too much of a fighter to give in easily,' Mrs Maxwell said.

'Sometimes it requires more strength to give in.'

'I hope you have the strength to give in to Mr Scott.'

Paula's head lifted sharply, but Mrs Maxwell stood her ground.

'I don't believe he only saw you in order to get you to drop those articles about his client.'

'There was more to it than that,' Paula retorted.

'Maybe. But you still haven't forgotten him.'

'He isn't an easy man to forget.'

'Why try? I know it's not my business, but—well—we'll soon be saying goodbye, and I feel that gives me the right to speak my mind. Don't let pride stand in your way, Miss Grayson.'

'It isn't pride, Mrs Maxwell, it's another woman.' She glanced at her watch. 'I must leave for my next meeting. I won't bother coming back afterward.'

'Do you need any papers?'

'All the figures I need are etched in my mind.'

'But there's nothing in your stomach,' Mrs Maxwell replied. 'You can't rush off without lunch.'

'It wouldn't stay with me, even if I ate it,' Paula said bluntly, and went into her private bathroom to wash and apply fresh make-up.

Warpaint for a woman who refused to fight, she thought

cynically, and wondered how different the battle would have been if Gregory had been on her side instead of Orian's. Always it came back to Gregory. She would never forgive him for using Lizbeth to spy on her in her own home.

'I hate him!'

She spoke aloud, then stared at her reflection and felt ashamed. Hatred would make forgetting him difficult. And forget him she must. Defiantly she applied more lipstick and walked out.

Paula's meeting with the Orian chairman took place in Morton Simmond's bank; this being considered the most suitable neutral ground. It was a grey stone building in a narrow turning off Moorgate, with simple uncluttered lines that gave no hint of the lavish interior, which had recently earned it two double pages in an art magazine of august pretensions. The boardroom was awash with Henry Moores and Paul Klees, and it was here, amidst an ocean of silver grey carpet, that Paula finally came face to face with John Gower.

He was an older, rougher edition of Gregory, and exuded an almost identical forcefulness of personality. She wondered how the two men got on. If like went with like, they must already be firm friends.

'I've been looking forward to this meeting, Miss Grayson,' he said. 'I'm glad our two companies are going to amalgamate with the minimum of fuss and publicity. When companies fight, a lot of people can get unnecessarily hurt.'

'It's people I'm concerned about,' she said, not wasting words. 'I wouldn't want any of my employees made redundant for the next two years.'

'Two?' he questioned.

'I wouldn't feel justified in stipulating a longer time.'

'It isn't our intention to make *anyone* redundant. We plan to expand Grayson Publications. A couple of years from now, you'll be wondering how to turn twenty-four hours into forty-eight!'

'Not me,' she said positively. 'I won't be remaining with the company.'

He looked astounded. 'But you've worked in the business all your life. You can't walk out and leave it.'

'I can and I will.'

'You think so now. But when you've had a rest—a long holiday perhaps—you'll feel differently. I know it's painful to give up a business you've always controlled, but——'

'My wanting to leave has nothing to do with that,' she put in swiftly. 'It's merely that I want to do other things with my life.'

His eyes, dark brown and bright as Gregory's, rested on her ringless fingers. 'Staying home won't occupy your mind, Miss Grayson. You've run a big business, and you'll want to go on doing so later if not sooner!'

'I won't rule out the possibility that I might return to Fleet Street one day,' she said idly, more to end the conversation than because she meant it.

'So that's it!' he said at once. 'You intend setting up on your own. What will it be, Miss Grayson? Specialised publications or a prestige Sunday paper?'

'I haven't given it a thought,' she protested, but saw he did not believe her.

There was no reason why he should, for his deduction was logical. Once you had printer's ink in your veins, you were a blue baby for ever. His suggestions weren't bad ones either. Small, bright monthlies and weeklies in which she could take a personal interest could be exactly the type of publishing she would enjoy. Excitement stirred and she drew a deep breath. Life was not over for her. She would still find fulfilling things to do.

'I'd still like you to stay with us,' John Gower said.

She shook her head. 'I want a different life.'

'You needn't work as hard,' he replied, misunderstanding her. 'Gregory Scott will be controlling the financial and legal side, so all you'll need to concern yourself with is the editorial.'

Paula was amazed. 'You mean he's giving up law completely?'

'He's cutting down on it. It's partly my doing,' he added. 'He has a brilliant brain and he isn't utilising it fully.'

'Not fully for *your* benefit,' she said wryly.

'Exactly!'

Paula placed Gregory in his new position and then thought of Guy. Somehow she could not see the two men working well together.

'What about the rest of my Board?' she asked.

'It will have to be pruned. Ardrey will stay, of course. He's a first class man.'

'He may not be willing to stay if Mr Scott's in control.'

'He never gave me that impression,' John Gower replied, marshalling the papers in front of him. He pointed to a column of figures and spoke to one of the young men at his side.

He had come into the meeting with three aides, all of them cut from the same mould: the better sort of public school and Oxbridge rather than redbrick. Mini tycoons, ready to be maxi ones when they had imbibed enough knowledge. Except that it wasn't only knowledge that made a tycoon, Paula thought, remembering her father, but flair and feel and ruthless guts.

She watched as two of the aides began leafing through their briefcases—as *de rigueur* a part of their uniform as their navy suits and white shirts—and wondered how John Gower knew that Guy would not object to working with Gregory. As far as she was aware, Guy had only met Orian's financial director once, many months ago, and long before either of them had known Gregory.

On an impulse that had no rational thought behind it, she said: 'I'm glad you appreciate Guy's ability. He's extremely clever.'

'You should hear him extol you!'

She shrugged. 'We've known each other for years.'

'I know. That's why I assumed you'd be willing to remain with us.'

'Even if I changed my mind about staying with the Group,' she said, 'I wouldn't be willing to work with Mr Scott. I don't appreciate his ethics.'

John Gower looked puzzled and Morton Simmons beseeched her with his eyes to hold her tongue. But why should she? She had been bought out and she was a free agent, able to say and do what she liked. At least let her get *some* pleasure from the situation.

'No one can fault Scott's ethics,' John Gower asserted. 'Mind you, I don't like using that word. It's come to mean too many different things.'

'To me it means integrity,' she said, 'which Gregory Scott is short on.'

'Really, Miss Grayson, I can't——'

'Miss Grayson and Scott were recently engaged in a legal battle.' Morton Simmonds slipped into the conversation with the fluidity of heated oil. 'And I feel she may still be smarting from it.'

'It has nothing to do with the Rossiter case.' Paula impaled the banker with an icy stare before focusing on John Gower. 'I can't say with certainty what I'd have done if I'd been in your shoes, but I'd like to think I wouldn't have made use of information that had been stolen.'

'Miss Grayson! I have no idea what——'

'Not all that dear,' she punned bitterly. 'Only today's valuation.'

Florid colour lessened the man's likeness to Gregory. But his mind was as quick, for he knew instantly what she meant. 'Scott had nothing to do with that. Nothing!'

'He's already admitted he had.'

'You must have misunderstood him.'

'I doubt it. He'll do anything to win a case and he's applying the same standards to business.'

'You're wrong, Miss Grayson.' John Gower stabbed the

air with his finger. 'You should look nearer home before you start accusing a man of Scott's integrity.'

On either side of him his young men were ageing by the second and Paula sensed their consternation. In their tight little world one did not rat on rats.

'Nearer home?' Ever the tidy banker, Morton Simmons picked up the pieces of the conversation.

'Come now, Simmons,' said John Gower. 'You can't expect me to tell you who.'

Morton's look told Paula that he agreed, but she was too determined to solve the problem to bother with the City protection racket.

'If Gregory didn't leak those figures to you, there are only three other people who could have done so: Guy Ardrey, his secretary or mine.' She looked at the Orian chairman. 'Guy never told me he had lunch with you. In the normal course of events he would have done so.'

'It probably slipped his mind.'

'You're too important to slip anyone's mind.' Her brain was racing like an engine, fired by the glorious realisation that at least Gregory was innocent of this piece of base treachery. 'By all means be discreet—I appreciate why you must—but it won't stop me from asking Guy myself.'

'My advice is to forget it. Don't look backwards, Miss Grayson. The future is far too exciting.'

'Not as exciting as the truth.' She rose and the men rose with her. 'Goodbye,' she said, and walked out.

CHAPTER FIFTEEN

PAULA had no conscious recollection of returning home. Only as she entered the library did she become aware of her surroundings, and then only because the telephone leered at her like a demon.

Picking it up as though it were Satan's tail, she dialled Guy's number. He answered almost as it rang, sounding jubilant as he heard her voice.

'Did everything go well, Paula?'

'Yes. I'd like to see you, Guy. Here. At once.'

Before he could question her, she put down the receiver, then restlessly paced around the room. She stared through the window, but it was too dark to see anything beyond the street lamps, and she passed the time by pouring herself a small whisky. She made a face at the taste, but the alcohol helped to steady her and when she finally heard Guy's voice in the hall, she was able to meet him with composure.

He had taken time to change into a lightweight grey suit, she noticed automatically, and wondered if he had done so after her call. Guy's wardrobe—he kept an extensive one in his office suite—caused great amusement to his staff, so Mrs Maxwell had informed her, for he had been known to change three times in one day: suiting the mood to the meeting, as one wit had put it: dark grey for a City lunch, heathery tweed to chair a meeting of newsagents from Scotland and black for a business dinner. Before she could guess what his particular change of clothes indicated, he went to kiss her.

'I was waiting anxiously for your call,' he said, appearing not to notice as she sidestepped his greeting. 'If you hadn't rung me, I'd have come over anyway.'

Silently she closed the library door and, alone with him, felt her composure disintegrate. Was John Gower right when he said she should look to the future and not hold post-mortems on the past?

She braced her shoulders and hit a straight left.

'Why did you give John Gower the revaluation figures on our properties?'

'You mean the bastard told you!'

Paula was too shocked to reply. Expecting denial, bluster, all kinds of pretence, she did not know how to deal with such raw confirmation. Reading her silence as a desire for explanation—as if one could explain the reason for treachery—Guy said quickly:

'I did it because it was the most sensible thing to do. Orian were determined to acquire us, and if they hadn't known the true value of our assets, they'd have put in a lower bid. You would have turned it down and we'd have had another battle on our hands.'

'Which you didn't want.'

'You know that. I've made no secret of my views.' He rubbed his hand across his face. His skin had a faint shine to it, as if he had broken out in a sweat. 'You would have lost the battle in the end and been exactly where you are now—except for a great deal more publicity and muck-raking. This way, you have a working relationship with Orian—if you want it.'

He made it sound so simple that she was almost fooled. But not quite. 'In the heat of battle we might have done better,' she said. 'We could have forced them to pay more.'

'Or frightened them off again,' Guy said quickly, his confidence returning at her steady tone. 'Selling out was the best way.'

'My father wouldn't have agreed with that.'

'Your father's dead. Believe me, Paula, I did what was best for the company—not for my personal ego. That was the trouble with your father. The company was his life—his other child, his first-born. He'd have clung to it even though he knew it was sinking. If he'd amalgamated with Orian five years ago—when he first had the chance—we'd be the biggest newspaper group in the world!'

She eyed him as if he were a stranger. 'You told him, of course?'

'No one could tell your father anything,' he said flatly. '*You* know that. Even *you* wouldn't listen to me.'

'So you took matters into your own hands?' Her temper was rising steadily.

'Selling to Orian is the best thing you've done. You'll

have a personal fortune and you can still stay with the company. Think of it, Paula: power without responsibility. It's what everyone dreams of. When you've had a chance to think it over——'

'I'll still despise you,' she cut in.

Her angry contempt hurt him and he rose to his own defence. 'I fail to see why. You've always said you wished you'd never inherited the company.'

'There's a difference between selling out and being sold out!'

'That's an unfair thing to say.'

'Was it fair to let me blame Gregory?'

'I tried to tell you you were wrong. I did my best to stop you from going to see him.'

'You did everything except tell me the truth,' she sneered. 'I wonder how he'll feel about working with you?'

Guy's colour remained high but so did his nerve. 'Men don't carry on feuds the way women do. In business, one fights the best way one can.'

'Even dirty?'

'Success is a great cleanser.'

Sickened, she turned away. 'Please go. I don't want to see you again.'

'You'll change your mind when you've cooled down. You're too intelligent not to see that I was right. I made nothing on the deal, Paula—I give you my word on that. I did it because it was the best thing to do.'

Gregory had done the same. Only his motivation had been to prove the innocence of a client. If she forgave Guy, she could forgive Gregory. But at the moment she could not forgive either of them.

'Please go,' she repeated.

For a long while afterwards she remained by the desk. Her anger at Guy's duplicity had given way to puzzlement at Gregory's reaction to her earlier accusation of him. His close liaison with John Gower made it inevitable that he

had known the identity of the person who had leaked the
valuation report, yet he had not told her, nor even hinted
at it, even though he had known that his silence would
confirm her belief in his guilt. It was inexplicable behaviour. Gregory was not the stuff of which martyrs are
made, yet on this occasion he had allowed himself to be
made one; had sacrificed his own good name in order to
save Guy's.

She had to have an explanation for it. Until she did, she
would worry over it like a ferret a rat. She gave a bitter
laugh; it was not the best simile to have chosen. She picked
up the telephone and put it down again. She was too tense
to speak to Gregory tonight. Her nerves were stretched to
breaking point and to conclude the day with another scene
was more than she could take.

On an impulse she could not check, she went up to Lizbeth's room. It faced her in pristine orderliness, as if no
angel-faced little scorpion had ever occupied it. How well
did Gregory understand the deviousness of that young
mind? Or didn't he care, as long as he had the young body?
Stifled by the thought, she retreated and closed the door.

She was crossing the upper gallery on the way to her
own room when she saw the butler going to the front door.
Pausing she watched him open it, then saw him swing it
wider.

Briskly a man's figure came into view and the controlled
violence of the stride told her at once who it was. She drew
back from the banisters, her heart thumping so loudly that
the voices speaking below her could not be heard. She saw
Gregory give a shake of his head and move further into
the hall, the action clearly indicating his determination to
wait to see her.

Reluctantly, though it was not evident in her firm step,
she came to the head of the stairs, lit there by the golden
radiance of wall-lights, as though she were on a stage.

'Paula!' He saw her immediately. 'I have to talk to you.'

She came down and led him into the drawing-room. It was larger than the library and she could more easily avoid being close to him.

'I took a chance that you would be here,' he said. 'I've just left John Gower and he told me what happened this afternoon. I'm sorry you found out about Ardrey.'

She could not think why, and tiredly rubbed at her forehead. 'I owe you an apology. I was—I intended calling you in the morning.'

'I haven't come here for an apology,' he said curtly. 'I have other things to say.'

'Not tonight. It's been a long day for me, Gregory, and I can't think straight.'

'Because you're upset. Being let down by two men in a matter of weeks isn't easy to take.' His mouth was a hard line. 'But at least when I planned to use you to prove Rossiter's innocence, I wasn't in love with you.'

Paula's stomach muscles tightened as if she had received a body blow. But Gregory did not notice her recoil and went on talking.

'Ardrey had no such excuse. He professed to love you, yet he was wheeling and dealing with John Gower behind your back.'

'He said he did it for the good of the company. That he didn't want me to fight the bid, and that he knew that if Orian's offer was high enough, our other shareholders would accept it and I'd be forced to give in.'

'Do you believe him?'

She swallowed. 'I don't see why not. He—he knew I found my position a strain, but that I wouldn't—that I'd find it hard to give it up, so he gave me the push I needed.'

'By a stab in the back!'

'That's your interpretation.' She avoided his eyes. 'Would you like a drink?'

'A what?' He caught himself up. 'Oh, by all means; as long as you don't ask me to drink to you and Ardrey!'

She went to the tray of drinks and with shaking hands

picked up a decanter. It rattled against the rim of the tumbler and some of the whisky splashed on to the tray. She was aware of Gregory watching her, but he made no comment on her clumsiness and silently took the glass from her.

'Have one yourself,' he said. 'You look as if you need it.'

It was easier to obey him than to argue and, with a tumbler in her hand, she sat down, choosing an armchair by the fireplace, with no chair nearby for him to take.

'Why exactly did you come here tonight?' she asked when the silence had gone on for a long time and it did not look as if he were going to break it.

'Because I knew you'd found out about Ardrey and I was concerned for you.'

'You don't need to be. I'm not a child, Gregory. I know how to look after myself.'

'You could have fooled *me*.'

She was too exhausted to spar with him. 'I don't want to appear inhospitable, but I'm not in the mood for conversation. It would be better if you went.' He made no move and she sighed wearily. 'You don't need me to explain why I suspected you.'

'I certainly don't,' he agreed, almost whimsically. 'You made it more than clear that you thought Lizbeth was my spy.'

'Can you blame me?'

He stared at her intently, his expression serious. 'No,' he said finally, 'I don't. In your position I would probably have thought the same.' He drained his drink at a gulp and went to pour himself another. Standing by the sideboard, he spoke. 'You already thought me a swine for the way I'd used you to prove my point over Rossiter—and I couldn't blame you for thinking I'd use Lizbeth for my own ends too.'

'You didn't deny it,' she reminded him. 'Why were you willing to take the blame for Guy?'

'It was the least I could do for you.'

Fresh as a daisy, she would still have found such an answer incomprehensible; fatigued as she was by this dreadful day, it was just a conglomeration of words that held no meaning.

'Could you be a little clearer, Gregory?' she said.

He drained his second drink and set down the glass, keeping his body half turned away from her. 'I don't think Ardrey's worth your treading on, let alone living with, but I couldn't bring myself to destroy your chance of finding happiness with him.'

The jigsaw puzzle became a picture and she saw how much he had hated himself for using her to try to clear Jack Rossiter's name. Hated himself enough to let his own name be denigrated.

'I ... I hadn't realised you were so self-sacrificing.' It was not what she had intended to say, but she was so afraid of giving away her feelings for him that even when she wanted to say something nice, it came out like an accusation.

'You still haven't forgiven me for Rossiter,' he said heavily.

'No woman likes being fooled.' Too late she remembered she was supposed to have done the same thing to him. 'You have my permission not to forgive *me*!' she said lightly.

'I think I'd be able to forgive you anything.' He swung round. Shadows had darkened the skin under his eyes and tiredness had etched the lines deeper on either side of his mouth. 'I never thought John Gower would tell you about Guy. God knows how you got it out of him.'

'He was defending *you*. He asked me to stay on with the company and I said I could never work with you.'

'There'd be no need. If you wish to remain, I'll leave the Orian Board.'

'That would certainly be a sacrifice,' she said without any sarcasm.

'I'll do it willingly.'

'No, thank you.' She braced herself for the lie she had to utter. 'If I really wanted to continue working for the Group your being there wouldn't make any difference to me.'

'I wish I could say the same. If you married Ardrey, I'd want to strangle you!'

'I have no intention of marrying a Judas!'

'If not him, then someone else. What the hell does it matter who it is?' he said savagely.

Exhausted though she was, Paula was too intelligent not to grasp the meaning his statement could hold. Could, but not necessarily did. There was still Lizbeth in his life. Very much in it, if the girl was to be believed. But she had to make sure.

'Lizbeth was delighted when you found her somewhere else to stay,' she said. 'I tried to make her feel at home here, but she wasn't.'

Gregory said nothing. Then he shrugged, as if accepting the change of conversation. 'Once we cut her aunt's claws, there was no reason for her to remain here with you. She wasn't happy.'

'She hasn't forgiven me for her father's death,' Paula sighed.

'There are other reasons,' Gregory said. 'She's jealous of you.'

'Only because she's young and not as sure of herself as she pretends. Once she's your wife she won't be jealous of any other woman.' Paula made herself smile. 'You should marry her soon, Gregory, and put her mind at rest.'

'I have no intention of marrying Lizbeth.'

Paula felt embarrassed. 'I'm sorry. I hadn't realised you were still keeping it a secret. She spoke as if....' Unable to bear him in front of her, she headed for the sideboard. But her head was already buzzing too much for her to take another drink and instead she toyed with a pair of ice tongs, moving them from one hand to the other.

'Would you tell me *exactly* what Lizbeth said to you about her relationship with me?'

Gregory spoke so quietly that Paula debated whether to shrug off the question. But as her shoulders moved, he moved too and came to stand beside her. The action told her he intended to have an answer and she had no option but to give him one.

'She said you've been in love with her for a long while and that you were—that you'd only realised it after her father had died.'

'You believed her?'

'Why *not*?'

'*Why not?*' It was an explosion of fury. '*You're* the reason why not! Don't you know how I feel about you? My God!' He reached for her, his hands heavy on her shoulders. Then one hand touched her chin, forcing it up until her eyes met his. 'You stupid woman,' he said in exasperation. 'Didn't you know she was lying? Are you so innocent that a child like Lizbeth could make you believe her?'

'She was. . . .' Paula swallowed. 'She was very persuasive. And you didn't exactly act as if you felt paternal towards her.'

'I don't.' A faint smile glimmered in the depths of his eyes. 'There may be a big disparity in our ages, but she never roused fatherly feelings in me—nor lover-like ones either. To me, she was the child of my closest friend; the little girl I'd watched grow up into a beautiful young woman. But I never thought of marrying her. I've never thought of marrying any woman other than you.'

Paula was dazed but not yet down. There were still too many needles stabbing at her. 'Why did you see her so often? She was always going out with you, acting as if— saying things that. . . .'

'To begin with I saw her because it meant I could see

you. I was still nursing the hope that I could cut out Ardrey. When I realised I couldn't, I went on seeing her because she needed me.'

'She's in love with you.' Paula was having no more dissimulation. 'She said you were lovers.'

Gregory's hands dropped to his sides, 'I love you, Paula. No one else. I haven't made love to another woman—nor wanted to—since the night I saw you at the opera. When I came to your office and discovered Paula Grayson was *you*, I forced myself to see you only as the head of Grayson Publications. I was determined to prove to you that facts were not always what they seemed.'

'And what were you going to do once you *had* proved it?'

'Spend the rest of my life proving how much I loved you.' A look of shame crossed his face. 'That night at the cottage I nearly told you the truth and to hell with my plan. I was all set to take you back to London, but you insisted we should stay.'

'What a fool I was!'

'A lovable, trusting one. If you knew how guilty it made me feel. . . .'

'Why didn't you tell me the truth *then*?'

'We got rather sidetracked on the sofa.' His voice was husky. 'I intended telling you the whole story the next afternoon. But that damned Mrs Anderson arrived first thing and the rest you know.'

How well she did; the sleepless nights, the tears, the anguish.

'You could still have come after me and explained,' she said.

'I wanted to give you a chance to cool down. You were so furious and hurt that I knew you were in no state to listen to me. Then, when we did meet, you said you'd only been seeing me because of Rossiter and that you were actually in love with Guy.'

She could not blame him for believing her; only blame herself for having acted so well. It should have been easy to tell him the truth now, but somehow it wasn't. Her thoughts about him and Lizbeth—even though she knew them to be untrue—still lingered.

'Lizbeth believes you'll marry her. She loves you very much.'

'The way a child loves,' he replied. 'Possessively and selfishly. That's why I found her a place with Jane. She'll be forced to mix with people of her own age and she'll soon see me as too ancient for her!'

Not for one moment did Paula believe him, but Lizbeth's feelings were no longer her concern. The girl had proved she could take care of herself and should now be left to do so.

'How could she have fooled you?' he went on. 'I thought you were too clever.'

'I fooled *you*,' Paula answered, 'and I thought *you* were too clever.'

Perplexity, memory and then realisation marked his features. 'You don't love Ardrey?'

'I never have. But how else could I save my pride?'

'When I think of the time we've wasted,' he muttered, and pulled her roughly into his arms.

His warmth enveloped her as he shakily stroked her hair and pressed kisses on her temple and cheek before finally finding her mouth. She parted her lips and savoured the scent of his skin. Her body trembled and she clung to him, glad when he supported her weight and drew her down on to a settee.

'We seem fated to love like this,' he said humorously.

'Don't be so pessimistic!'

There was a surging movement in his body and his grip was painful. 'Oh God, Paula, if you knew the sleepless nights you've given me!'

'That's all over now.'

'Don't you believe it,' he said upon her mouth. 'They're just the beginning. Will you marry me, Paula Grayson?'

'You'd have a job stopping me, Mr Scott.'

Best Seller Romances

Next month's best loved romances

Mills & Boon Best Seller Romances are the love stories that have proved particularly popular with our readers. These are the titles to look out for next month.

FRUSTRATION
Charlotte Lamb

HELL OR HIGH WATER
Anne Mather

WITH THIS RING
Mary Wibberley

Buy them from your usual paperback stockist, or write to: Mills & Boon Reader Service, P.O. Box 236, Thornton Rd, Croydon, Surrey CR9 3RU, England. Readers in South Africa-write to: Mills & Boon Reader Service of Southern Africa, Private Bag X3010, Randburg, 2125.

Mills & Boon
the rose of romance

Best Seller Romances

Romances you have loved

Mills & Boon Best Seller Romances are the love stories that have proved particularly popular with our readers. They really are "back by popular demand." These are the other titles to look out for this month.

MARRIAGE IN MEXICO
by Flora Kidd

Sebastian Suarez had rescued Dawn from drowning off the coast of Mexico and then done her a further favour — which was why she had accepted his proposal of marriage. But it didn't take her long to fall in love with him — nor to realise that he had married her only as a smokescreen to conceal his affair with another woman...

DECEIT OF A PAGAN
by Carole Mortimer

When Templar's sister had a baby by Alex Marcose and then both she and Alex died, Templar took the child herself. But Alex's forbidding brother Leon didn't know all this, and naturally had the lowest opinion of Templar — an opinion that didn't prevent him marrying her for baby Keri's sake. How could Templar tell him the truth now — when it would mean his taking the child away from her?

Mills & Boon
the rose of romance